RUNNING FRO

The Gilbert Girls, Book Two

by Cat Cahill

Cover design by EDH Professionals

ISBN: 978-1096652977 (paperback)

Chapter One

Crest Stone, Colorado Territory – 1875

Thomas Drexel was lucky.

Or at least he had been lately. He was lucky that Monroe Hartley had hired him back in Denver, when all he needed was to get out of town as fast as possible. He was lucky the work paid well. He was lucky hardly anyone ever came to this hidden valley. And even when the hotel burned up all his hard work over the summer, he was lucky they needed to rebuild and kept him on.

He hoped his luck would hold now. It was either that or go to California or Mexico—someplace no one would ever think to look for him. He pulled off his hat, smoothed down his sun-streaked hair, and knocked on the door of the McFarlands' apartment.

Mrs. McFarland answered, rosy-cheeked and smiling as always.

"Good morning, ma'am. I work—or worked, really—on the building crew. I'm Thomas Drexel. I'm wondering if I might have a word with your husband?"

"You must be hungry," she said by way of inviting him in.

"No need to trouble yourself." He inched in, feeling six kinds of awkward in her well-kept home. Thomas hadn't seen the inside of it since he'd helped install the wood trim a few weeks ago. As the hotel manager and the bookkeeper, Mr. and Mrs. McFarland were appointed a three-room apartment on the first floor of the hotel.

"Nonsense," Mrs. McFarland said with a warm smile. "Do sit. I'll fetch Mr. McFarland and some hotcakes and bacon."

Thomas's stomach rumbled at the very mention of bacon. The building crew usually made do with a stew of venison or rabbit and, if a man had enough time to make a trip to Cañon City, some cheese or bread. It had been nonstop work since the hotel had burned in early August. Now, finally, it was all completed and due to open to guests tomorrow.

"Thomas!" McFarland entered the room. He had seemingly transformed overnight from a grizzled bear of a man who'd worked on everything from repairing the existing buildings across the tracks to fetching supplies in town to a gentleman with slicked-back hair, neatly trimmed beard, and, of all things, a suit.

Thomas blinked for a moment, trying to sort out what he saw. "Good morning," he said a bit stiffly.

McFarland laughed. "Surprised how I cleaned up?" he asked in his Irish brogue.

"No, sir." Thomas recovered quickly. He had a large favor to ask, and insulting the man wasn't exactly the best way to begin.

Mrs. McFarland arrived at that moment with two plates of hotcakes and bacon and two mugs of steaming coffee. It was perfect timing, both for the potential awkwardness of the situation and for Thomas's stomach.

After they'd both eaten their share of breakfast and discussed the state of the new hotel, Mr. McFarland asked, "What brings you to see me? Aside from my wife's cooking, that is."

Thomas drew in a breath. "I'm hoping that after the crew is dismissed today, I might stay on. I could do any sort of work. Carpentry, as you know. I'm good with horses and livestock. I can repair just about anything. I can fetch necessities from town. Anything you might need."

"Can you cook?" Mr. McFarland asked.

Thomas nearly choked on his coffee. "I . . . well, I can learn. I'm a quick study."

McFarland laughed again. "I'm joking. We have enough kitchen boys." He set his coffee on the lovely hand-carved low table. "You've been a good worker, Thomas. I could certainly find something for you to do here, but I'm curious why. You could find better-paying work with the building boom up in Denver, especially now that you have experience."

Thomas wasn't prepared for this question, but he quickly formulated an answer. "I like this place, this hotel. I feel at home here." He hoped that was enough to avoid any more questions.

McFarland nodded. "I've been here a while myself, since the days of the railroad camp. There's something about this valley."

Thomas murmured in agreement, even though he hadn't really thought of it that way. He just needed to stay here, out of sight, tucked away in this valley where no one knew who he was.

McFarland was watching him. "Of course, I was also sweet on this girl whose family had a small ranch a few miles away."

Thomas's thoughts instantly flicked to the pretty blonde girl he'd first noticed at Hartley's wedding a couple of months back. Since that time, he'd seen her now and then—fetching food from the springhouse at the creek behind the hotel; making her way across the railroad tracks and the hill that stood between the new hotel and the old white house where she'd been living with the other girls; laughing as she entered the rebuilt hotel for the first time. He swallowed. The last thing he needed was McFarland suspecting him of breaking the rules with one of the Gilbert Girls, especially when he'd never so much as spoken to her. The hotel's restaurant waitresses were strictly forbidden, if a man wanted to keep his position with the Gilbert Company. "There's no girl."

The man kept his eyes on Thomas a moment longer, then nodded. "All right. If you want, you can start right away. The head chef has already requested more shelving in the pantry. Speak to him and find out what he wants."

"Yes, sir. Thank you." Thomas shook McFarland's hand and made his way back through the hotel toward the kitchen.

The large hotel lobby was mostly empty, save for a couple of new men behind the front desk and a more travel-weary man in front of it.

"Sir, I don't know if we're allowed to post those," one of the new hotel employees said.

"Then I'll wait for your boss." The dusty man in front of the desk dropped the saddlebags from his shoulder to the floor. He must have traveled all night to get here so early.

Thomas slowed his pace, eyes fixed on the front doors of the hotel but ears trained on the conversation at the desk.

"Go on," the traveler said to the man behind the desk. "'Lest you prefer scofflaws and murderers roaming free."

Out of the corner of his eye, Thomas could see one of the desk clerks move quickly toward the wing that housed McFarland's apartment.

Scofflaws and murderers.

Thomas swallowed hard and yanked his hat down farther over his eyes before sliding out one of the imposing front doors into the sunlight.

His days here might be more numbered than he'd thought.

Chapter Two

Crest Stone, Colorado Territory

Caroline Beauchamp surveyed the hotel's dining room for the millionth time that morning. She wanted to ensure each table was at least two feet away from its neighbors, the floor was spotless, and the tablecloths showed not a single wrinkle. Somehow it calmed her to do things such as this. Speaking of the tablecloths . . .

She pinched a corner of cloth and examined it a bit more closely. These would need to be pressed again today. She'd be certain to let Mrs. Ruby know after the morning meeting. One by one, the other girls streamed into the dining room, some yawning, others almost bursting with excitement. Penny and Dora, two of Caroline's first friends upon arriving in Crest Stone, made their way through the newer girls.

"Can you believe it's nearly here?" Penny's eyes sparkled and her entire body hummed with an excitement Caroline could feel.

"What if we make a mistake?" Dora asked. She twisted her hands together.

Caroline took one of her hands. "You won't. You've been training for this for months now. And it isn't so different from bringing the guests sandwiches onboard the train." Since the hotel and restaurant had caught fire in early August, which had delayed its opening, Mrs. Ruby had decided it would be most efficient and welcoming to make sandwiches and deliver them onboard the train cars to the waiting passengers as they traveled south to Santa Fe and north to Cañon City.

Dora shook her head. Dark tendrils of hair wisped around her smooth, olive-skinned face. "It's not the same. This is so much more . . . formal."

"Don't fret about it," Penny said. "You know what you're doing. Now these other ninnies, I'm not so sure . . ." She waved a hand at the larger group.

Caroline scanned their faces. She spotted Millie and the three girls she'd arrived with halfway through the summer. And then there was a sea of exactly twenty-three other girls, most of whom had come just before the fire. Since that time, the newer girls had been living in canvas tents, which the building crew had kindly vacated until the Gilbert Company had sent a shipment of canvas. Caroline and her friends were the lucky ones—they'd been able to remain in their rooms at the old house. But last week, all the girls had moved into their dormitories inside the finally completed hotel. There was only one girl missing from the group.

"I wish Emma were here," Dora said quietly.

"As do I," Caroline said. "But I wouldn't take her happiness from her."

"She's off having grand adventures." Penny's face nearly glowed, as if she wished she were in Emma's place.

"I don't know how adventurous the California desert is," Caroline said. Emma had arrived with the three of them in late May, making their foursome the first Gilbert Girls in Crest Stone. But she had since married Monroe Hartley, the hotel's builder, and after staying to oversee the reconstruction of the Crest Stone Hotel, they had moved on just a couple of days ago to build another Gilbert Company hotel in California.

"Oh, but it is," Penny said. "Just think! Snakes, outlaws, scorpions, no water for miles and miles."

"That sounds horrifying," Caroline replied.

Dora nodded in agreement.

"You wouldn't know adventure if it knocked you in the head, Caroline Beauchamp. Why—" Penny's words stopped when Mrs. Ruby walked into the room.

"Good morning, ladies." Mrs. Ruby's voice boomed across the large room. "This is a day of last-minute preparations. I want you all to inspect your clothing, check your stations, and ensure the tables are spotless. Now that the hotel will be opening, twice-daily trains will begin stopping tomorrow at noon and six p.m. If you feel the need to practice serving today, then by all means, please do so.

"Please note that I'll be observing all of you over the next few days to select a head waitress and an assistant head waitress. In those positions, you will be privy to all decisions made regarding the dining room, you will be consulted regarding the hiring of new girls, you'll be in charge of the dining room when I am not present, and—of course—your pay will reflect your new role. You are dismissed."

The girls immediately began chattering among themselves as they broke off to attend to their duties.

"Excuse me," Caroline said to her friends, who were already talking about who they thought could be named head waitress and assistant head waitress.

Mrs. Ruby was just finishing up answering a question for one of the newer girls when Caroline approached her. "Miss Beauchamp?"

"Mrs. Ruby, I was examining the tablecloths before you came in, and I believe they may need to be pressed again. They seem to have acquired a fair amount of wrinkles." Caroline reached for the nearest cloth and held up the end to show Mrs. Ruby.

The older woman squinted at the material and nodded. "Excellent work. The housemaids will need to press those before morning. I'll alert them." She paused and looked Caroline over from head to toe before nodding in satisfaction. "I trust you were paying attention to my announcement?"

Caroline nodded. "Yes, ma'am."

"You have continued to prove yourself worthy of the Gilbert name. I see a great future for you in this company." With that, Mrs. Ruby moved faster than one would suspect a woman of her size could toward a group of girls congregated near the door to the kitchen.

Caroline's entire face went warm. Could Mrs. Ruby have been suggesting Caroline might be named head waitress? The thought made her arms and legs feel almost too light to work. Never had she thought she would come this far. When she'd arrived here in May from Boston, she'd felt like a tiny, timid mouse about to be buried under the sheer *emptiness* of this wild place. Everything had frightened her—Mrs. Ruby, the men building the hotel, the miners a few miles east, the sharpness of the mountains to the west, the way the sky seemed to go on and on, the lack of any comfort she'd had in the city. More than once, she had determined to resign herself to what awaited her if she returned to Boston, because at least that was familiar, even if it was what she'd run away from.

But she'd been lucky to make quick friends here. At first, Penny, Dora, and Emma didn't know why she'd left Boston without telling a soul. What they did see was a girl who was capable of living up to the work expected from a Gilbert

Girl. With their encouragement, Caroline worked and worked and worked, until she'd become proficient at chores she never would have even contemplated at home.

A smile tugged at the corner of her mouth as she wondered what her delicate older sister and her prim mother would say if they knew she could serve a table in under thirty minutes or wash her own clothing or—even worse—start a roaring fire to stay warm. That latest skill was newer, now that the nights had turned particularly chilly. Even the days had grown cool enough to require a coat on occasion. Snow had already come to the mountains above them, and according to Mrs. McFarland, it wouldn't be long until snow found its way to the valley as well.

Caroline didn't mind snow. She had learned she didn't mind hard work either. She felt useful here, unlike at home. There, she'd often imagined herself a prized sow to be trotted out at dinners and parties to eligible young men. Here, at Crest Stone, in this little valley surrounded by friends, she felt . . . *alive*. Free. Capable of providing for herself. Able to make her own decisions. She would never give that up.

All she had to do was remain hidden here.

Chapter Three

Thomas bit down on the nail between his teeth as he lined up the notches he'd cut in the two pieces of wood. If he was honest, he'd admit he'd never made shelving before. But surely it couldn't be that hard. After all, he'd helped build a hotel—twice.

The notches didn't line up. He spat the nail at the workbench he'd dragged out of the shed behind the hotel. He needed a break before his annoyance boiled over into anger.

Although if he were being completely honest, it wasn't just the shelving that was fouling his mood. It was the man from earlier, the one with the wanted posters.

Thomas reached for the dipper in the bucket of cool water he'd pulled from the creek before he started working. While there was a chill in the air, the sun was still bright, and something about that made him thirsty. Or maybe it was the fear that his face was on one of those posters inside the hotel lobby right this moment. Or the guilt at what he'd done that ate at him if he thought too much about it.

He pulled off his hat, reached for another ladle of water, and dumped this one over his head. Dropping the dipper back into the bucket, he rubbed at the cold liquid trickling its way through his hair and into his eyes. That did the trick. His mind sharpened just enough to remind him that he didn't necessarily know there was a sketch of him in that sheath of paper. After all, wouldn't one of the front desk employees have recognized him and sent McFarland after him? Although it hadn't even been an hour yet . . .

A woman emerged from the kitchen door, interrupting his worried thoughts.

And not just any woman. She was the one who'd caught his eye more than once since Hartley's wedding.

Her arms were filled with a wooden crate of glassware, and she kicked the kitchen door shut with her foot. She set the crate down next to one of the fussy wrought-iron chairs that someone had pulled from the nearby garden. Then she settled herself onto the equally fussy floral cushion and reached into the crate. She pulled out a piece of stemmed glassware and began rubbing at it with a cloth.

Thomas couldn't take his eyes off her, and she hadn't even noticed him.

Eventually he realized he must look a fool, standing there, covered in sawdust, water dripping down his shirt, and staring at this girl who looked as if she'd blown in on the breeze. He shook his head and clamped the worn brown hat back on it.

The shelving. He needed to get back to this project, or else McFarland would have no use for him.

Rather than waste the wood he'd already worked with, he decided to trim off the notches on each piece and try again. This one could be a smaller shelf to hang just inside the door for those items used most often. He began to saw into the wood, letting the misshapen notches he'd made earlier fall to the ground.

"Pardon me." A higher-pitched voice sounded over the grind of metal through wood. "Pardon me!" it said again as he yanked the saw through the last bit of wood.

He looked up, knowing exactly whom he'd find in front of him.

And he wasn't wrong.

The petite blonde girl stood in front of him, one hand on her hip, the other one holding out a delicate glass. She wore the soft gray dress and white apron that all the Gilbert Girls wore under a black cloak, and a small, matching gray hat perched on her head.

"Good morning, miss," he said as he pulled off his hat and ran a hand over his wet hair. His words were smooth, but his heart leapt in a strange way to see her this close to him.

"Good morning," she said shortly. "Would you mind terribly if I asked you to relocate your . . . woodworking?"

She looked a bit ruffled, and something about that delighted him. But he schooled his face into an impassive expression. The last thing he wanted was for this beautiful woman to think he was laughing at her. "How come?"

The woman held out the glass. He looked at it, but all he saw was, well, a glass.

She shook it a little in her small hand. "You're getting sawdust in the stemware."

He stepped around the workbench and peered into the glass. One tiny piece of sawdust sat on the side of the glass. He reached in, pressed it against his finger, and lifted it out. "Fixed," he said, holding his finger out to the girl.

She stared at his hand as if he held a dead mouse in his palm. "You dirtied it! Now I have to wash the glass and let it dry before I can rub the spots off it." Her words were so carefully formed, almost as if she were speaking to the queen of England and not a man born and raised in Texas by a barkeep father. He had only scant memories of his mother, but according to his father's tales, she would've gotten along well with this pretentious fussbucket of a girl.

The way she kept looking so appalled at his hand made it impossible to keep the laughter in. It burst out like a rush of wind. "I apologize for sullying your glassware. But to be truthful, no one is going to notice one tiny piece of sawdust in a glass."

She drew herself up to her fullest height, still nearly a foot shorter than Thomas. Wisps of wheat-colored hair floated around her face and her blue eyes shot fire at him. "The Gilbert Company does *not* serve its guests from glasses with even the tiniest speck of dust, sir. Now will you kindly move your bench away from my work area?"

He couldn't keep the grin off his face. She was livid. That only made him want to poke at her more, almost to see if she'd drop her high-society facade. "No, ma'am. I don't believe I can. You see, I set up here first—at the request of the head chef—and here I intend to stay. You'd best find yourself a new place to scrub at your glassware or just get used to filling it with *all* of this sawdust."

The girl's face went bright red. "I—" She didn't finish, only clamped her mouth shut and spun on her heel back to her chair.

Thomas laughed to himself as she picked up her crate and marched away toward the garden. She was awfully pretty, he had to admit as he picked up a knife and the recut piece of wood. Beautiful, in fact.

But far too prim for his liking.

Chapter Four

Caroline scrubbed at the glass much harder than was necessary. *That man. How dare he?* she thought for about the tenth time since she'd relocated her work from behind the kitchen to the now-dormant garden behind the ladies' parlor. Just thinking about how infuriating he was made her hands shake as she picked up another glass. No man in Boston would've ever treated her so. Not that she particularly liked the way they handled her as if she were a piece of this stemware, prone to snapping apart at the slightest tremor. But at least there had been respect, and politeness, and . . . and . . . She was so angry, she couldn't even think straight.

It wouldn't be so bad if she didn't keep finding her eyes drifting toward him every other minute. She thought she recognized him from the building crew, but those men had all but left. Perhaps he was here to handle loose ends, such as carpentry that blew into her work. Her temperature rose yet again as the man whittled away at a piece of wood, his attention focused completely on his work. She was too far away from him to tell for certain, but he appeared intent, pulling his hat off and leaving it on the ground. His warm blond hair was ruffled and just a tiny bit too long. It would make Caroline's mother recoil in horror. *Barbaric,* she could almost hear Mother's voice in her ears. For some absurd reason, it made her smile, particularly as he absentmindedly ran a hand through it, messing it up even more. Certainly no man in Boston wore his hair in such disarray.

A bird of some name—Caroline could never tell the difference—chirped overhead, reminding her that she was staring at this most irritating man and shirking her duties. She hurriedly wiped clean the glass in her hand and picked up the next. Spending hours daydreaming instead of cleaning glassware was not the path toward demonstrating she was the best choice for head waitress.

Caroline pressed her lips together as she worked and tried to ignore the infuriating man a few feet away. *Head waitress.* She'd hardly thought she'd be in this position just a few months ago when she was fumbling through the simplest task and wondering if she'd lost her mind completely. Her success so far was due entirely to the support of her friends. Without them, even the burning desire to never set foot in Boston again wouldn't have been enough to keep her from giving up in those early days.

She held a perfectly clean glass up to admire in the sunlight. It was pleasant enough out here, provided one could ignore impertinent men. The days had turned cool, but not yet cold, the air was crisp and refreshing, and the creek hidden behind the cottonwoods and pines made a pleasant enough gurgling sound. The lovely green and golden leaves of the aspens and cottonwoods, with the snowcapped mountains rising behind them, distorted in the curve of the glass, making Caroline smile.

The abject terror she'd felt arriving at such a remote place last May had tempered over the months. She had to admit this valley had become home. She was safe here, far away from family who would have her do their bidding, from the commitment she'd felt she had no choice but to make, from a society that would never comprehend why she wouldn't do as she was told, and from a man who scared her even more than the thought of bears in the brush or outlaws carrying her off in the night. It was as if this valley had reached its arms around her and hidden her between its mountains. And she had made something of herself here. She was no longer Miss Beauchamp, daughter of an import company king and Boston society queen, educated in the finest manners and skills befitting a lady of her station. Here, she was simply Caroline Beauchamp, a woman who could support herself, a friend, and someone who could perhaps move up in the Gilbert Company.

She placed the glass with the others and reached for yet another one, as the sound of metal sawing into wood drew her attention back to the man to her left. He was a hard worker too, that much was clear from the effort he expended on the work in front of him and the fact that while the rest of the building crew was gone, he was still here. She wondered at his age. At first, she hadn't thought him much older than her own newly turned eighteen years—perhaps in his early twenties—but when she'd stepped closer, she wasn't so certain. He had a world-weary look about him, almost as if he'd seen more than most men and hoped to forget it.

He paused to wipe his face against his sleeve, and Caroline wondered what he had seen, where he was from, and why he was here. He seemed at ease out here in this valley, as if he were used to the wilderness. Of course, it could have grown on him, as it had on her. Given that he'd had to saw off work he'd already done to redo it, she doubted he'd had much experience in carpentry. How was it, then, that he'd found himself on a building crew?

At just that moment, he glanced up and caught her eye. A half-smile creased his face, and she looked away as fast as she could, her heart pounding. *Foolish*, she scolded herself as she reached for another glass. Here she was wasting her time staring wistfully at a man in a most unladylike fashion—a man who'd been nothing but rude to her. She was far better off pretending he wasn't even in the vicinity. She should focus her thoughts on the task at hand and on convincing Mrs. Ruby she would be the perfect candidate for head waitress.

She had nothing but hope for her future, and spending a second's thought more on the man a few feet away from her would only derail her plans.

Chapter Five

The haughty blonde woman finished her work about half an hour after she started. Thomas watched her return to the kitchen with her crate of glasses even as he told himself good riddance. He didn't know what he had hoped she would be like when he'd first seen her—gentle, perhaps, but quick to laugh—but she certainly didn't meet that ideal. It was just as well. The last thing he needed right now was a woman, particularly one he wasn't even allowed to speak to on anything but the briefest of hotel matters.

He worked for the rest of the afternoon, stopping for a brief bite to eat in the kitchen from the grateful chef. Just as the sun began to sink, he finished the last shelf. It was good timing too, given both the loss of light and the increasing chill in the air. He delivered his work to the pantry. He'd hang the shelves tomorrow morning before the first trainload of passengers arrived at noon. After returning the equipment to the shed, he made his way to the hotel lobby.

What might be in there now had been on his mind all day. He'd hoped—and even prayed, though he wasn't certain God listened much to men like him—that McFarland had sent that man with the posters packing. Or perhaps the poster he dreaded wasn't in the man's bag. Thomas hadn't exactly made himself scarce all day, and yet McFarland hadn't come looking for him. That could only bode well, he hoped.

He entered the lobby from the hallway that led back to the kitchen and the ladies' parlor, hoping that would be less conspicuous than opening one of the large front doors. The hallway had been quiet, and when he stepped into the lobby, only one man stood behind the front desk, scratching out something on a scrap of paper. Thomas nodded at him when the man paused to dip the pen. The man nodded back, and Thomas dared to hope that this was also a good sign.

Scanning the room, he found the posters hanging near the entrance of the men's smoking parlor and the room that housed the hotel's lunch counter, off to the left of the front desk and not too far from the hallway where he'd entered. The clerk had gone back to his writing after acknowledging Thomas. When he paused by the posters, he was out of the clerk's sight. He drew in a deep breath and clenched and unclenched his fists before letting his eyes rove across the papers tacked neatly to the fine wallpaper.

Bandits, murderers, train robbers. These men were the worst of the worst. His eyes stopped on the last poster. There, a crudely drawn image of himself glared back at Thomas. It wasn't a perfect match, but it was close. The artist had gotten his eyes wrong and made his nose too crooked. The hat he wore in the picture was one he'd lost months ago. It was close enough to be him, but only recognizable to someone who really took the time to see his features. But the best part—the one that lightened his heart more than he'd dared to hope since he'd come here—was the name. Nowhere did it say *Thomas Drexel*. Instead, it read, *Tom the Cat, Wanted for Robbery and Murder of the Sheriff of Barrett Mountain. $700 Dead or Alive.*

He swallowed hard. They'd upped the reward *and* given him a nickname. Tom the Cat. It had a good ring to it, if he was inclined to such things. He wasn't, though, not in the least. But he'd gladly take the nickname if it kept him anonymous here. No wonder he'd been left alone all day. Between the imperfect picture and the nickname, no one had put it together that this was him. Smiling, he took a step backwards—straight into someone.

A little squeak sounded from the woman he'd run into. Thomas turned around and yanked off his hat. "I apologize, miss," he said, his eyes alighting on the slight blonde woman who had given him such trouble earlier in the day.

But she didn't speak. Instead her gaze went from him directly to the bottom poster on the wall. Then back to him. She tilted her head, then her eyes widened.

She knew.

Chapter Six

Caroline couldn't keep the tiny squeal from her voice as the man wrapped his hand around her arm and fairly dragged her into the smoking parlor.

"Unhand me, you—you—" Every word that came to mind wasn't one she could speak in polite company. Although here she was, alone in a room with a man whose image was on a wanted poster, so she supposed she was hardly in polite company. She'd run away from Boston to escape a man whose very gaze made her tremble, despite his genteel outward appearance, and now she found herself alone with someone who was wanted by the law for murder, of all things. If she wasn't so terrified, she'd laugh at the absurdity of it all.

He let go, but only to quickly close the door to the room.

Caroline's heart pounded wildly. "How dare you? Open that door immediately!" When he made no move to do as she asked, she moved toward the door herself.

The man's hand darted out again and grabbed her by the wrist. She tugged against his grip, but he refused to let go.

"Remove your hand!" she demanded, pulling again. "Or else I'll—"

His other hand clamped over her mouth. It wasn't rough, but it startled her all the same. Fear snaked its way through her entire body. She couldn't move. She was frozen there against a dark leather wing chair, alone with this . . . this *murderer*.

The man's eyes went soft as they searched her face. They were a blue-gray color and looked nothing like the artist's depiction. These eyes were kinder, less wild, and more haunted. The second the thought crossed her mind, Caroline chided herself for being ridiculous. Murderers didn't have kind eyes.

"Just let me speak," he finally said. "Will you do that? Please?"

His voice wasn't threatening at all. In fact, he sounded almost scared. No one had ever been scared of her, and the idea made Caroline's heart slow just a little. This man—as rude as he was earlier—hardly seemed like an outlaw.

She nodded, and he dropped his hand from her mouth, taking with it a warmth she hadn't noticed until it was gone. She pushed her lips together and tried not to think about how he still held her wrist in his other hand.

"That poster makes me out to be someone I'm not."

"You didn't kill someone?" Her voice trembled as she spoke.

"It was an accident. I was working up in the mine at Barrett Mountain. My job was to collect the pay for the whole camp from the narrow gauge. It was just me and the camp sheriff. He told me the boss wanted me back down at the mine. I didn't believe him, because there were always at least two of us with the money at all times, and usually three. When I refused, he drew, I followed suit, and . . ." He finished, his eyebrows drawn together as if he was begging her to believe him.

And did she?

Caroline wasn't certain. She wanted to. As angry as he'd made her earlier, now he seemed vulnerable and almost . . . nice. "Why didn't you explain the situation?"

"No one would've believed me. It was my word against the sheriff's. I didn't run right away. I hid out nearby, long enough to overhear he didn't die immediately. He was alive long enough to tell the company officials and his deputy I killed him in cold blood to steal the money. And . . ."

Caroline waited a beat for him to finish. When he didn't, she prompted, "And?"

He closed his eyes a second and swallowed. "The money had disappeared. Someone else took it, and it wasn't me. But it sure looked as if I'd done it. So I left."

"You came here," she said softly. If what he said was true, her heart ached for him. *If* what he said was true, that is.

"I came here." His eyes found hers and held them, almost pleading with her to understand.

Caroline stilled, everything in her coming to a stop as he held her gaze. She couldn't think. Time paused as they stood there. It could have been seconds or hours for all she knew. Then, as fast as it had happened, it ended as he seemed to realize he still held her wrist in his hand. He let her go, his fingers brushing against her skin in a way that made her shiver.

"Do you believe me?" he asked.

She breathed in and out a few times, trying to piece her thoughts together and ignore the lingering shadow touch of his hand on her arm. Did she believe him?

"I want to," she confessed. "But . . ." Her heart thudded as she uttered the last word, and a brilliant—if not dangerous—idea came to mind. If he truly was guilty, he wouldn't let her leave this room. If she was brave enough, she could find out whether he was lying. She said a quick prayer that he was not before drawing up all the strength she'd gathered since she arrived here. It wasn't much, but it would have to do. She held on to the arm of the chair for support. "It's quite a story, Mr. . . .?"

"Drexel," he supplied. "Thomas Drexel."

She nodded. Politeness dictated she give him her name in response, but again, politeness hardly covered situations in which one found oneself inappropriately ensconced in a room with a man who was an accused murderer. "Mr. Drexel. I believe the best course of action now is to find Mr. McFarland and let him know your . . . story."

The light went out of his eyes, rendering them a sad, lonely gray. It reminded her of the bay back home in March. "You don't believe me," he said. "I should've known."

Chapter Seven

"What do you mean?" she asked.

He gestured at her, as if it were written across her clothing. "You're so . . . proper. I know how women like you are—convinced the world should revolve around you. Fussy to the point of—" He clamped his mouth shut, forcing the desperation down somewhere deep inside. This woman held his life in her hands. Insulting her wasn't exactly helping his cause, even though he could recount the litany his father told of his mother and it would fit this woman perfectly.

She drew herself up taller, which, to his amusement, was still nearly a foot shorter than he was. "I beg your pardon?"

He berated himself silently. "I apologize. I meant only that you seem the sort to do the right thing."

Her pretty blue eyes narrowed, and she crossed her arms. He supposed she thought it made her look determined, but in truth, she looked like an angry porcelain doll. Her features were so finely drawn, it was impossible for her to appear harsh. She was beautiful, simply put. Beautiful and judgmental. Likely as selfish as every other woman with money. He'd do well to remember that.

Although . . . if she had money, what in the name of all that was good was she doing here, working as a waitress at the ends of civilization? His mother had never lifted a finger in her life, preferring instead to wait for funds to arrive from her family back East when his father failed to earn enough to purchase whatever frivolous items she wanted.

"Of course I'll do the right thing," she said. "I was raised properly. Unlike yourself, it seems."

Thomas bit back a smart reply. She had no idea how he was raised, and she could shove her preconceptions right back down where she'd found them. *Your life is in her hands*, he reminded himself. And so he remained silent.

"Right." She nodded, almost as if talking to herself. "I'll go get Mr. McFarland. Will you be here, or should I presume you'll run again?"

He hesitated. What he wanted to do was grab hold of her and talk the truth into her until she believed him wholeheartedly. But how would he do that? Force her to stay in this room against her will?

Perhaps his time here was up. He'd been here nigh on five months, longer than he'd ever thought he could get away with when he arrived. Maybe he should cut his losses now and leave. He could take his chances in California, or ride for Mexico. That's what he should've done months ago, anyhow. No one would find him in Mexico.

To be honest though, he hated to leave this place. Mr. McFarland was right. These mountains, this valley, the work—it had worked its way into his bones. Leaving would be like ripping out a rib.

Lose a rib or lose his life. The choice was clear, as much as he hated it.

"Do what you need to. I'll be here," he finally said.

The woman lifted her eyebrows, almost as if this was not what she'd expected him to say. One hand brushed wisps of hair that fell about her face, and a slight flush of pink crept up into her cheeks. For someone holding his life in her hands, she looked quite vulnerable.

He pressed his lips together and took a step back, as if that would make her somehow less becoming.

"I'll return in a moment," she said as she made her way to the door.

It closed behind her, and Thomas made himself wait a full minute before launching himself toward the door. He had taken one step when it opened again. He jerked to a halt. Had she found McFarland that quickly? He'd have to think of a new plan, and fast.

But when the woman slipped inside, no one else followed her.

He took another step forward, eyes searching her face as she gathered her hands in front of her. Her fingers twisted together, almost as if she was nervous about what she would say. He paused and waited for her to speak.

She closed her eyes for a couple of seconds as a slight shiver made her body shake. Thomas clenched his hands into fists to fight the strange desire to reach out and take her into his arms. Finally, her eyes landed on his face.

"I believe you," she said, her voice so quiet he had to lean forward to hear it.

He blinked at her. This made no sense. "What's your game?"

"My what?"

"Why did you leave to find McFarland just now, and then turn around and tell me something completely different?" The blood rose into his face as he spoke. Was she baiting him? But how? And why?

She lifted her chin and pushed her shoulders back. "Mr. Drexel, I assure you I have no such 'game.' I simply changed my mind when I realized you weren't stopping me from going to Mr. McFarland. No guilty man would have let me leave. Therefore, you must be innocent of the accusations on that poster."

Her words were like a slap in the face. She watched him earnestly, honesty pouring out of her. This woman was no snake-in-the-grass saloon girl. She might be full of herself and believe she reigned superior over him and anyone else who came from a background that wasn't moneyed, but she appeared as if she truly believed she was doing the right thing. Meaning . . . she believed him. The guilt that sat in the back of his mind reminded him that didn't make him any less a murderer, no matter his intentions. He'd taken a life, and he'd live with that knowledge for the rest of his own.

But this woman at least believed he'd had no choice.

Just as quickly as he'd become angered, Thomas settled. His hands softened and he relaxed. "Thank you, Miss . . .?"

She hesitated, her eyes roaming his face.

"I could call you Miss Fuss, but I imagine you'd prefer me to use your given name." The second the words were out of his mouth, he wished he could take them back. Although the way she bristled again, all indignant and full of fire, was enough to make him glad he'd teased her.

Provided she didn't change her mind again.

Her jaw set, as if she was holding back every word she truly wanted to say to him. He wished she would speak her mind, but she was too well-bred for that sort of thing.

"You may call me Miss Beauchamp." She nearly ground the words out through her teeth, then must have realized how she sounded as she forcibly relaxed her face. "My decision comes with one condition, though."

He cocked his eyebrows. "Pray tell, what is your requirement, Miss Beauchamp?" He sounded overly polite, which made her narrow her eyes at him again. He choked back a laugh. It was easy to ruffle this woman's feathers, and he was getting far too much enjoyment out of doing so.

"I want you to confess your situation to Mr. McFarland yourself."

Thomas kept his face immobile as he let her words sink in. There was no way he could tell McFarland he was on the run, not if he wanted to keep his position here, and especially not if he wanted to keep out of the hangman's noose.

Chapter Eight

Mr. Drexel studied her for a moment, almost as if he was weighing her request. Caroline held her breath, praying he'd agree. He had no choice, really, but she hoped he was the sort of man who'd prefer to set things right on his own terms.

Finally, after what seemed like an hour, he nodded. "I'll do as you request."

Her heart soared. "I'm so happy you agree."

"You didn't give me much say in the matter," he said with a half smile. "I don't know how he'll take it. I may be out of work and in a jail cell by tomorrow evening. I don't suppose you'll visit me?"

Caroline's face went warm as an iron. He was awfully forward, particularly for a man in his position. Yet somehow, images of her bringing him packed lunches while he was behind bars flitted through her mind. What was wrong with her? Her face grew even hotter, and she ducked her head as he chuckled.

He was utterly maddening. She forced herself to look up at him, ignoring the state of her flushed face. "That would be most inappropriate, sir. And I doubt Mr. McFarland will call for your arrest. I imagine he'll want to help you after he hears your tale."

"I don't know about that, but how about you send up a prayer for me?"

Caroline smiled tentatively. She hadn't pegged him as a religious sort of man. "Yes, of course."

"Thank you." He held her gaze a moment too long, and she found herself glued in place, a million thoughts flooding her head. What if she were free to be courted? What if she didn't have a family she was certain was actively looking for her? What if she didn't need this job to survive?

No, even if she weren't burdened with her past, she *wanted* to be a Gilbert Girl. She'd worked so hard to get to where she was, and now she might have the opportunity to become head waitress. That meant more pay, more responsibilities, more of a name for herself within the company. She couldn't—wouldn't—risk it all on a rough-edged man wanted for murder. The very thought was ridiculous.

"Let me see if anyone might be in the lobby before we leave." Mr. Drexel was still looking at her, and, she suspected, was trying to figure out what was bothering her so. Let him think it might be her reputation. After all, it certainly should be.

She nodded, and he went to the door, cracking it just wide enough to stick his head out, and then opening it farther. "Even the desk clerk has gone for supper," he said, sweeping his hand in front of him to usher her out the door.

Caroline complied after checking her hat and brushing her hands down her skirt. She stopped just outside the door, in front of the wanted posters. Mr. Drexel's penciled face stared back at her with different eyes and a wider hat. She reached out for it, then stopped. "Why don't you remove it?" she asked him. "After all, if you're confiding in Mr. McFarland tomorrow, it's no use having someone recognize your face before you have a chance to talk to him."

He looked at her as if he wasn't sure he heard her correctly. Then he gave her a wide smile and yanked the page from where it lay pinned to the wall. He crumpled it up and shoved it into a pocket.

Caroline returned his smile. "Things will work out well for you, I just know it."

"I hope you're right," he replied.

She glanced over her shoulder toward the stairs that led to the upper floor. "I bid you good evening, Mr. Drexel."

He bowed his head just slightly, and even as she wondered at this unexpected courtesy, he said, "Would you like me to escort you upstairs?"

The smile dropped from her face as she took a step backward. How dare he? "Absolutely not."

His laugh followed her all the way up the stairs as her face burned. At least no one was in the lobby to have heard what he said. The man was completely hopeless.

As she made her way down the long hallway that led to the girls' dormitories, a tiny sliver of doubt worked its way into her hope. Had she done the right thing? He was wanted for murder, of all things. It wasn't as if he'd stolen something—he'd killed a man. Back in Boston, there would've been no question about what she would have done. She'd have immediately fetched her father or her older brother, and they'd have contacted the authorities. And she never would have seen the ruffian again.

Although, she had to admit to herself as she reached the door to the room she shared with Penny, she never would have met such a man in Boston to begin with. Her social circle had been tightly kept there. That was part of what drew her to this wild place. It had taken some time to get used to, but now she loved that everyone she met wasn't automatically wealthy and concerned with appearances or business deals or family names.

She took a deep breath and forced Mr. Drexel and any doubts from her mind. When she opened the door, three pairs of eyes greeted her. Penny sat, looking into the small glass they kept at their dressing table, repinning her hair, and crowded onto her bed were Dora and Millie, who shared a room at the end of the hallway.

"Where have you been?" Penny asked, her eyes alight.

Caroline bit her lip. Penny would *love* to hear about Mr. Drexel and his plight. This was the sort of thing she lived for. But the man's life hung in her hands, and Caroline wasn't about to betray that trust, particularly when he'd agreed to do the right thing tomorrow. Instead, she leaned over Penny's shoulder to check her own reflection and said, "Just ensuring our stations are perfect and ready for tomorrow."

Millie laughed. "I *knew* you'd go after that head waitress position."

Caroline smiled at her. It had taken Millie a while to find joy in life again after that horrible Mr. Turner had taken advantage of her affections this past summer. But now Millie seemed to thrive in her work and had become a friend to every girl in the hotel.

"I don't deny I'm interested. But of course, there's no telling who Mrs. Ruby will deem worthy," Caroline said as she shoved thoughts of Mr. Drexel from her mind.

"Oh, don't you worry about that," Penny said as she pinned her hat into place. "We'll make sure she knows you're the only choice. Won't we, girls?"

The other two nodded, and a wave of happiness rushed over Caroline. How had she been so lucky as to find such good friends out here? "Thank you so much. It would mean the world to me if I won that title."

"It's no bother," Penny said. She stood. "Now, we have fifteen minutes until supper, and Dora needs to tell us all about that desk clerk who said hello to her earlier."

Dora's complexion deepened to a dark red, and Caroline smiled in sympathy. Once Penny got a hold of gossip, she reveled in it. So as much as Caroline wanted to confide in her friends about Mr. Drexel, she knew she couldn't. At least not until he'd cleared his name.

She sat at the dressing table, letting the girls' chatter wash over her. Tomorrow, she'd seek out Mr. Drexel again to find out what had come of his meeting with Mr. McFarland. She'd have to be sneaky about it, which she hated. But it was necessary if she wanted to keep her position.

Losing her work here as a Gilbert Girl was not an option.

Chapter Nine

Thomas awoke at dawn, wondering at first why it was so comfortable in his tent. Until he realized he was no longer in the tent. He had taken it down yesterday in preparation for the hotel's grand opening, and McFarland had assigned him a room on the upper floor in the rear of the hotel where the male employees of the Gilbert Company had dormitories.

He stretched and sighed, enjoying the comfort of the feather mattress and the general lack of chill in the room. He had no roommate, but that likely wouldn't last long as McFarland still needed to hire a few more people. Or, he thought with a grimace, because he'd no longer be here himself.

His clothing from yesterday was thrown over a chair in the corner. He had one other shirt, which had been laundered the day before yesterday. When he next received his pay—provided he still had a job and wasn't in jail—he would go to Cañon City and purchase some new clothing. Even if he wasn't working directly with guests, he decided it would be wise to take more care for his appearance.

There was a small looking glass next to the washbasin. Thomas picked it up and frowned at what looked back at him. He needed a haircut, too. Badly. Once, a long time ago, he'd thought he'd follow his father's unrealized dreams of opening a store in a town somewhere. He didn't know what sort of store, nor did he particularly care, but the idea of spending his days talking with the various sorts of people who'd come in appealed to him. As did the thought of being his own boss and running a business as he saw fit. His father had saved for his own store for years, only to pass on before he could fulfill his dream. The money had then gone to pay the undertaker and rent they'd owed the landlord for the last couple of months. Thomas had used the meager remainder to make his way out of Texas, to the promised lands of silver mines in Colorado.

Of course, those promised lands never quite lived up to their reputations. It was far too easy to spend one's entire earnings on company food and company rent. And as he hated to admit, on the sins such a place offered. After six years of working the mines, Thomas had nothing to show for it except a warrant for his arrest.

He threw water on his face, hoping it would drown all those old memories. He combed back his hair as best he could before putting on the clean shirt and grabbing his hat.

The kitchen was open early, and both men and women filled the long tables at the end of the room, eating a quick breakfast of eggs, bread, and ham.

"Good morning, Drexel." A hand clapped his shoulder, and he stood from his seat at the end of the table to find McFarland behind him.

"McFarland." He shook the man's hand.

"I trust you slept well?"

"I did, thank you. Do you need a seat? I'm just finishing."

"No, no." McFarland waved a hand, indicating Thomas should sit back down.

He didn't, of course. Instead, he stood there while the promise he'd made Miss Beauchamp knocked on the corners of his skull. Now was neither the time nor the place, and besides, he wasn't entirely certain he wanted to keep the promise to begin with. He grimaced at that thought. Never had he been a man who told falsehoods. Although if he were being honest with himself, his entire existence for the past five months had been a falsehood.

"The missus made certain I ate a hearty breakfast before she'd let me leave our apartment." McFarland placed a hand over his large stomach and laughed.

"I'm about finished with the pantry shelving," Thomas said, shoving Miss Beauchamp's voice and trusting face from his mind. "I only need to hang it."

"Good! I knew you'd waste no time. Why don't you find the smithy once you're done? I believe he's needing some repairs to his building."

Thomas nodded. He knew the place. It was one of the old railroad company buildings scattered on the other side of the tracks.

McFarland went on to shake other hands and give encouragement for what would certainly be a busy day. Thomas was glad to make himself scarce from the hotel before noon, when the first train was due in. He installed the last shelving unit around eleven, just as the meal preparations in the kitchen for the incoming train guests hit a frenzy.

The kitchen had set out a hunk of cheese and some bread for the hotel's employees to grab their noon meal on the run. Thomas wrapped some in brown paper, thinking he'd take it outside where he could watch the train come in. While trains had been regularly passing Crest Stone for the past two months, this would be the first one to allow passengers to disembark.

He pushed open one of the doors that led from the kitchen to the dining room. Women in dove-gray dresses with crisp white aprons and matching white hats scurried to and fro. It caught Thomas off guard for a moment, and he paused, right outside the door.

It only took a few seconds to spot Miss Beauchamp. She was busy moving place settings a fraction of an inch at a table near the wall. The promise he'd made rose to the forefront of his mind. He'd agreed because he'd had no choice. What else could he have done? Women with money believed the world acted according to their whims, so trying to convince her otherwise would've been useless.

You convinced her of the truth. He batted away the inconvenient reminder. That was a different situation.

What he needed was proof. This wasn't the first time he'd had that thought, but it somehow seemed more urgent now that Miss Beauchamp was involved. Proof that would convince the authorities his own life had been in danger, that the sheriff was the one who'd tried to steal the company pay, and that someone else had actually stolen it after he'd run. But what might that proof be? And how would he get it?

He huffed, frustrated yet again that there wasn't some obvious solution. However, Miss Beauchamp didn't need to know that. Maybe he still had a chance to stay here, to convince her he couldn't tell McFarland just yet.

"Sir? Sir!"

A woman with hair the color of fire stood in front of him, her hands on her hips. He yanked off his hat and nodded at her.

"Sir, you can't be in here. Kitchen help is forbidden from the dining room during mealtimes." She ran her eyes over his once-white shirt, worn pants, and dusty boots, as if trying to figure out what exactly it was he did in the kitchen.

"I'm not kitchen help, miss," he said, looking past her to where Miss Beauchamp had finally noticed him. Her eyes widened, and he was sure he'd caught just the hint of a smile before she ran her hands over nonexistent wrinkles in her apron.

"Still, you can't be in here! Mrs. Ruby will have the vapors if she sees you in here. That is, if she doesn't slap you first." The red-haired girl was so put out by his presence, he couldn't help but laugh.

"Then by all means, I'll show myself out." He strode purposefully through the dining room instead of returning to the kitchen, feeling almost as much as seeing Miss Beauchamp's frown.

He didn't know why he so enjoyed getting a rise out of her, but as he shut the front door of the hotel behind him, he knew he should stop. Nothing good would come of teasing that woman. In fact, she might get the wrong idea, and while the thought of her falling for him was unlikely, it certainly wasn't impossible. After all, his mother had seen something in his father, enough to make her leave her wealthy family and move to a dusty cattle town in Texas where she'd then made his life anything but happy.

No, nothing good could come of teasing Miss Beauchamp.

Chapter Ten

"Remember, thirty minutes, girls. Pleasant, but quick." With that reminder, Mrs. Ruby retreated to the corner of the dining room where she could oversee her charges.

Penny squeezed Caroline's hand before running off to wait on her first customers. Train passengers dressed in traveling clothes were beginning to stream through the open dining-room doors. This was it. This was everything they'd been working toward for months. Caroline drew a deep breath and swallowed the fear that had risen in her throat. There was no reason to be nervous. She was well-trained. All she needed to do was prove to Mrs. Ruby that she could be head waitress.

With a smile on her face and her hands demurely clasped in front of her, Caroline made her way to the couple seated at her first table.

"Good afternoon. My name is Miss Beauchamp." Despite all the months of training, it felt incredibly forward to introduce herself in this manner. But the couple merely smiled at her and introduced themselves as Mr. and Mrs. Foster of New York.

"I'll bring your soup momentarily. Would you prefer the venison or the pork for your main meal? Each is served with roasted potatoes and carrots from our garden." She was glad she was already smiling, or else she would've broken out into one for correctly remembering the options and side dishes.

The couple both ordered the pork, and Caroline scurried off as politely as possible to alert the kitchen and retrieve their soup. When she returned, soup bowls in hand, the rest of the tables in her section had been seated. There was another older couple and three tables of single men. The man at the table farthest from her looked up, and Caroline nearly dropped her soup bowls.

She yanked her gaze from him to deliver the soup, pasting a smile back on her face. As she made her way to the next table, she chanced a glance up.

The man was looking down at his water glass, which he'd already drained. She couldn't be certain from this angle, but he looked so much like the son of one of her family's neighbors in Boston.

It couldn't be, could it? It was so unlikely.

But she had to know for certain. She welcomed the older couple and took their orders, then went straight to the man in question. He looked up as she drew closer and . . .

Caroline nearly grabbed the empty chair at the table in relief. It wasn't him.

The remainder of the thirty minutes flew by. Caroline rushed to and from the kitchen and the water station with the other girls. She successfully fed all of her customers before they needed to return to their train cars. After cleaning up her tables and righting them for the next train, which would come through at six o'clock sharp, she threw on a cloak and a pair of gloves and escaped out the back door of the kitchen.

By now it was nearly midafternoon. The sun shone and nary a cloud was in the sky. The October chill was precisely what she needed after so much hard work. She wanted to find her friends and see how their work had gone, and she would, but not now. After the scare she'd had and the sheer energy of serving so many people so quickly, she needed time alone.

The creek gurgled behind the tree line as she followed the old wagon path that led to the water. Mountain springs fed the creek, which was shallow this time of year. An old spring house stood nearby, soon to be replaced by a new, larger one. Caroline stood and let the cool air wash over her, trying to empty her mind and enjoy the scenery. But it was no use. The fear that she could have been discovered the very first day the restaurant opened overtook her.

How many more times would this happen? How many scares would it take before someone she knew from her old life appeared at the hotel? The hotel had wire service now. Once someone discovered her, it would be no time at all before her family was alerted to her whereabouts. And then what?

Tears leaked from her eyes even as she yanked off her gloves and swiped them away. They should just leave her alone. To take the dire action she did to get away from them, one would think that would be message enough that she never wanted to return. But that was impossible. Her father had never been foiled in business. Why would he let his own daughter ruin his plans?

To make it even worse, she missed them. How one could despise and miss her family at the same time made no sense at all. But it was true, and just thinking it set another wave of tears cascading down Caroline's face.

"Did the frogs request dinner service?" Mr. Drexel appeared from nowhere, it seemed.

Caroline turned her face away, shoving her gloves into her skirt pocket before scrubbing at tears with the heels of her hands. The last thing she wanted was this man seeing her so vulnerable.

"What happened?" he asked, the teasing grin slipping from his face.

"Nothing. Please leave me be."

"Was one of your customers cruel to you?"

Caroline glanced at him. The man had his hands clenched and his jaw set, almost as if he were ready to run off and challenge some imaginary rude customer to a brawl. For her.

"No, nothing like that. It . . ." She wiped at her eyes again as she tried to figure out how to tell him without relaying her entire story. She was not a liar, so some kernel of the truth would simply have to do.

"Take your time," he said, his voice softer than usual.

She swallowed hard. "There was a man at one of my tables who resembled someone I knew at home."

He waited.

"I- I don't wish for anyone from Boston to know I'm here." She forced herself to keep her eyes on his.

He wanted more, she could tell, but he was too polite to ask. Somehow that reassured her. The man wasn't completely without any social graces.

"And was it the man you knew?" he asked.

"No." The relief flooded through her again, and new tears sprang to her eyes as the fear of what *could* have happened rushed back to her mind. No matter how fast she scrubbed them away, more came.

Mr. Drexel took a step forward, and then another. And then he was there, right in front of her, holding a handkerchief. She took it gratefully and pressed it to her eyes, but the tears wouldn't stop coming. Her body shook as she imagined everything she'd worked so hard for here crumbling as her father forced her back home. Back to a man she never wanted to think of, much less see, again.

"There, now." Mr. Drexel reached around her with both arms, and she sank gratefully against his chest. "You're safe. No one knows you're here."

Another great sob racked her body, but he didn't let go. After a moment, Caroline's tears slowed. She clutched his drenched handkerchief in one hand, while the other, she realized with growing alarm, was flush against his chest. She went completely still as she sniffed.

What had she done?

Chapter Eleven

Caroline's body went stiff against him. Thomas immediately dropped his arms, letting them fall to his sides. She took a step back, her face still flushed pink from crying.

"I'm sorry. I shouldn't have done that." He braced himself for a tongue-lashing.

"Thank you," she said with a raw voice. And that was all. No lectures on propriety, no reminders that they shouldn't be here alone together, no righteous indignation. Just a simple *thank you*.

He pulled at his vest, straightening it. "You're welcome."

She was watching him with soft eyes, almost as if something about him had changed in her mind. "Mr. Drexel, I apologize for becoming so emotional." She ran one hand over her hair, as if smoothing it would erase what had just happened.

He smiled. She'd shown him she had a soul buried under those proper layers. He wasn't about to forget that. "Please, call me Thomas."

Her eyes widened, and her hand fluttered back down to her side. "I couldn't."

"You just spent several minutes weeping against me. If that doesn't allow us to call one another by our Christian names, I don't know what does."

The ghost of a smile lifted the corners of her lips. "I suppose you're right. I'm Caroline." Her eyes traced the ground, almost as if she were too shy to tell him her name.

Caroline. It was like a song. "It suits you," he said.

"Thank you." She glanced back up at him, her face a little more pink than it was before, and looking nothing like the entitled woman he'd do well to remember she was.

He nodded and cleared his throat.

"Tell me, Thomas," she said, and if he'd thought her name was like a song, hearing her say his was quite possibly the most beautiful melody he'd ever heard. He'd never been musical himself, but one of the few memories he had of his mother was of her singing him lullabies. As a child, he'd thought it was the most wonderful sound in the world, even though now he knew it had come from a cold-hearted woman.

"Yes?" he said, forcing his mind back to the present.

"Were you able to speak with Mr. McFarland?"

He stilled, acutely aware of every sound around him as he fumbled for an answer. A chickadee chirped somewhere in the trees above them, the shallow creek gurgled its way south, someone laughed near the hotel past the tree line, and a faint clanging sounded from the smithy shop. The latter reminded him he still had work to finish today.

"Thomas?" she said again.

"I haven't," he finally replied, "but for good reason."

Her eyebrows lifted, and it felt as if something heavy had fallen in between them.

He shifted his feet and hoped she would understand why. "I need proof. Something to prove that the sheriff intended to steal the money, and that someone else actually did. Something to prove I acted to defend myself. Else why would McFarland believe me?"

Caroline's eyes narrowed. She was pondering his words. For the second time in two days, he prayed.

"I believe you without proof," she said. "Although I had the distinct advantage of testing you."

He held his tongue, letting her arrive at her decision without interference. He only hoped it would be the right conclusion.

"How do you intend to find this proof?" she asked.

This was the hole in his plan. "I don't know yet. I should have looked before now, but I was too afraid that if I did, I'd be found. So I didn't. But now . . ." He wanted to say he was tired of hiding, tired of living in fear that the next train would carry a lawman who'd arrest him on the spot, tired of having his name—his father's name—muddied with these accusations. He owed his father more than *this*.

"You want freedom," Caroline said, her voice almost a whisper. "I understand that."

"Will you help me?" he asked before he even realized what he was saying. Had he lost his mind? "I'm sorry. I shouldn't have asked."

Caroline nodded. "No, please don't apologize. I don't know what I can do, but if I can help you, I will."

He smiled, and for the first time in months, it was unencumbered. If that was how being free from all of this would feel, he wanted it more than he'd ever wanted anything.

Caroline pulled his handkerchief between her fingers, and then glanced down at it, almost as if she'd just realized she was still holding it. "I'll see that this gets laundered and returned to you."

"No, please keep it."

It was as if a shadow crossed her pretty round face, and he could almost hear her saying that it was inappropriate for her to receive a gift from him. But instead, all she said was, "Thank you." She glanced back through the trees, toward the hotel that was hidden from view. "I'm glad to help you, but it must remain between us."

"I understand. I'm well aware of the rules." Even the hotel's builder had lost his job because of his relationship with one of the waitresses. He'd only gotten it back when he married her.

"Thank you," she said, "for everything." She exchanged the handkerchief for a pair of gloves from a pocket in her dress. "I must return to my duties. I've been gone too long."

"Of course." He took a step back to allow her to pass. "I'll wait a few minutes before I return."

She gave him a grateful look. "This work means everything to me."

Thomas nodded, although as she disappeared back up the wagon path, he tried to piece together the riddle of this woman. It now made sense why she was working here—she was hiding from her family. He was certainly curious why, but what confused him most was how seriously she took her work. With her background, he'd have assumed she'd try to latch on to the first moneyed man she met out here. Perhaps Caroline had only meant that the work meant everything to her in the temporary sense. After all, one had to eat to remain alive.

She'd now have plenty of wealthy suitors from whom to choose, now that trains were stopping regularly at the hotel.

And yet, he still couldn't see her throwing herself at some man only because he had money.

She was a puzzle, this woman. She'd even agreed to help him search for proof to exonerate himself, and while he'd hoped she'd agree to keep his secret for a while longer, he'd hardly expected her to help him. He hadn't even planned to ask.

As he returned to the hotel, he wondered what else there was to Caroline Beauchamp.

Chapter Twelve

"Excellent work today, ladies!" Mrs. Ruby beamed at the lines of Gilbert Girls assembled in the dining room late that night. "You all worked hard to make today a success. Please be certain to get enough rest tonight. Mr. McFarland?"

Mr. McFarland's smile matched Mrs. Ruby's. Their pleasure made Caroline's heart swell. Her feet hurt, her back ached, and her stomach rumbled with hunger, but she'd never been happier. All of her train guests had been served in under a half an hour, and the few guests staying on at the hotel had enjoyed a leisurely meal later in the evening. She didn't have to be present for breakfast in the morning, and for that small gift, she was grateful. Still, she radiated with pride at what she'd accomplished today.

"The Crest Stone Hotel and Restaurant is off to a stunning start," Mr. McFarland said, his hands clasped behind his back. "We have twenty-two guests tonight, but know that number will increase as more trains come through. I'll see you all tomorrow."

With that, Mrs. Ruby dismissed the girls. Caroline slumped a little in relief.

"I plan to sleep until noon," Penny said, stifling a yawn.

"You'll miss the lunch service," Caroline reminded her.

Penny groaned and linked elbows with Caroline. "Do you suppose they'll notice if I sleep while I serve guests?"

Caroline laughed. "Only if you spill the coffee."

"I have to report for breakfast at six," Millie said as she and Dora joined them outside the dining room. "I don't know how I'm going to make it!"

Dora nodded in agreement, although to Caroline, she looked about half-asleep already. If the girls served breakfast, they'd receive the evening meal off, while the opposite also held true.

"Oh!" Penny exclaimed, hardly appearing tired at all now as they passed the open door to the small lunch counter right off the lobby. Guests who couldn't afford the dining room, or who preferred to have a simpler meal, could come to the lunch counter for cold sandwiches or soup. "Did you hear that Genia dropped a tray of soup all over the lunch counter this afternoon?"

"It only splashed a little on the countertop. It mostly hit the floor and didn't get on any customers," Millie corrected.

"Still," Penny said, her eyes wide. "Can you imagine the talking-to those girls received from Mrs. Ruby?" She shuddered. "It had to be worse than when I burned a hole through one of her dresses."

Caroline couldn't help but laugh a little. Penny's general ineptitude with anything related to housekeeping outshined even Caroline's troubles with it toward the beginning of their training. Over the summer, they'd learned both housekeeping and cooking skills so they could help Mrs. Ruby train the maids and even the kitchen boys when they started arriving just before the hotel's originally scheduled opening date. It was hard work, harder than anything Caroline had ever done in her life, but she'd grown to love it. She didn't necessarily love all the chores they'd practiced—she'd be thrilled if she never had to scrub another pot encrusted with burnt food again—but she reveled in the fulfilled, exhausted, *useful* feeling she'd had at the end of each day. She was pleased to note that she still felt that way, even now that her duties were more narrowly concentrated on serving guests.

She was drifting behind the others as they reached the top of the stairs. Penny and Millie still chattered, while Dora looked ready to collapse where she stood. A sudden movement from the doorway that led to the library caught Caroline's eye. Certain it was one of their guests looking for reading material, she had almost looked away when Thomas's face appeared around the open door.

Caroline nearly gasped as he drew back inside. Her heart thumped as she scrambled for a reason to go into the library. The girls were allowed to borrow books, but saying she wanted one might mean one of the others would join her. Maybe she could have forgotten something downstairs . . .

"I fear I've left a letter in the kitchen." Caroline patted the pocket of her skirt for effect.

"Do you need company?" Dora asked, yawning.

Caroline smiled. "No, I'll be quick. You go on to bed."

"Are you certain?" Millie asked. "Remember what Mrs. Ruby said."

Caroline remembered. Mrs. Ruby had warned them against wandering the hotel alone at night. While they hoped their guests were of the highest quality, no one knew for sure. After all, the hotel hardly checked references when guests arrived. "I'll be quick," she said. "Besides, we have only a handful of guests, and it's been quiet now for at least an hour."

Millie nodded, appearing reassured. Caroline slowly made her way back toward the stairs, but when her friends rounded the corner to the hallway that led to the women's dormitories, she paused. After waiting a minute or so, she turned and strode toward the library.

"This is most improper," she whispered the moment she entered the room. A single lamp burned low where it sat on a mahogany table. Thomas had most likely brought it with him, as the only lights in the room were the lamps affixed to the walls, and none of those were lit.

"But our rendezvous by the creek was proper?" His eyes glinted with mirth in the yellowish light. "I seem to recall your clinging to me as if I were a single tree in a storm."

She wanted to slap him. Gone was the tenderhearted man she'd seen this afternoon. The teasing cad had returned. "If you're only here to remind me of what a . . . a scoundrel you are, then I'll bid you good night."

"A scoundrel? Lady, you offend me." He held a hand to his heart in a mocking impression of someone who actually cared about what she thought of him.

Caroline let out a small huff and began to move toward the door. If he could do nothing but tease her, then she had nothing better to do than retreat to her room for some sleep.

"Wait." He grabbed hold of her wrist.

Caroline stopped and turned. He immediately dropped her arm, and a tiny part of her wished he hadn't. She must be exhausted to be thinking so. "Am I here for a reason or simply to entertain you?"

His grin dropped into a more serious expression and his gray eyes went somber, betraying a sadness Caroline hadn't seen before. The moral weight of what he had done whirled through her head. She couldn't imagine existing each day knowing she had been responsible for another's death. Her heart ached for him.

"I apologize," he said. "I was hoping you might have a few minutes to help me."

Any trace of the day's fatigue hid itself beneath the nerves that began humming under Caroline's skin. "I might. How could I help?"

"I thought it might be best to give you the facts of what happened the evening I . . ." Thomas closed his eyes briefly. Of course she didn't know what he was thinking, but it seemed to her as if he still had a hard time admitting what he had done. Maybe that was the only way he could live with it. "Then perhaps we might figure out how to obtain proof of my innocence."

Caroline nodded. "All right." She settled herself into a stiff-backed chair at a small table. The larger, plush wing chairs looked far more likely to cause her to fall asleep.

Thomas joined her, sitting in the second chair at the table. Then he began.

Chapter Thirteen

Thomas leaned forward in his chair, resting both hands on the fine wooden table. The piece, like most of the furniture in the hotel, had been shipped from back East. Only the massive front desk downstairs had been created on-site through the hard work of many men on the crew. Thomas ran the facts through his head, trying to determine the best place to begin.

Caroline remained still, her eyes on him. She was far more patient than he'd thought she be. Most women of her status would have already been nattering on about another subject, but she waited.

"It was late in the evening," he finally said.

She nodded at him to continue.

"I'd been working at that mine for a couple of years. I'd been entrusted with a number of jobs that the bosses and the men who worked in the office didn't care to do. And one of those jobs was transporting the pay. It had to be emptied from a strongbox on a railroad car into another box we brought on a wagon, which we then drove back to camp. When I got to—"

Caroline held up a hand. "Was the box locked?"

"Yes. We carried pay for every man in the camp. We couldn't risk it being stolen."

Caroline nodded again, her eyes narrowing just a little. It was almost like a tell. Narrowed eyes meant she was thinking, not necessarily that she was angry or that she didn't believe what he was saying.

"Normally, I'd go with another man and the sheriff the company employed. It took two of us to load the lockbox, and the sheriff kept watch in case of trouble. That day, it was just me and the sheriff. I had no reason to suspect anything was wrong about that, since it had happened once or twice before. We'd loaded the money and had gotten to the outskirts of the encampment on our return. It was maybe a quarter mile from the railroad line, but there were quite a few trees so you couldn't see the tracks from the camp. We got to the fork in the road that led to the mine one way and the camp the other when the sheriff asked me to stop."

"How come?" she asked.

"He said the mine boss had told him to send me to the mine after we'd fetched the pay. I told him I had to see the money to the company office first. That was my job. He insisted that I get out and he'd drive the wagon the rest of the way. This was where I became suspicious. Part of the reason more than one person went to transport this money was to keep it safe. No one was supposed to be alone with it. I informed him it was my duty to ensure the men's pay reached the office. He insisted the boss had asked him to bring it instead. He even insinuated the boss had suspicions about me."

"Did he?" Caroline asked. She leaned forward, hands still in her lap, as if he were telling the most riveting tale she'd ever heard.

"Of course not. Why would he? I was a loyal employee. I'd never caused trouble before. Well, not while on the job, at least." He gave her a wink. She frowned disapprovingly at him, which made him laugh. "I attempted to get the horses moving again, and that's when he took a swing at me. I fought back. I'll, uh . . . I won't go into the details of that," Thomas said when an appalled look crossed her face. Did men not fight in Boston? He supposed they simply threw their money at each other to solve disagreements, instead of their fists. Give him a good, honorable fistfight any day.

"Did anyone see this?" she asked.

"No. We were well-hidden because of the trees, and most of the men were down at the mine. No one came until . . ." He paused. He was jumping ahead. "I'd finally wrested him from the wagon—after he'd broken my nose, by the way." He paused a moment to let that sink in. Despite the gravity of his situation, he was rather proud of that fact. But when Caroline showed no degree of being impressed, he continued. "The sheriff drew at that point and demanded I go down to the mine. I refused. I couldn't afford to lose that work, and I most certainly would be let go if I didn't deliver the pay. So I did the only thing I could think to do. I dove under the wagon. That threw him off long enough that he didn't fire right away. By the time he did, I was half out the other side, and he missed by a wide berth. The moment I was out, I drew and returned fire.

That bullet got him in the stomach. That's when folks finally showed up. Just in time to see me with the pay wagon, and the sheriff shot on the ground."

Caroline drew in a breath. "That's . . . unfortunate."

He gave a dry laugh. "That's one word for it."

"How did you break free?" she asked.

This was the part he dreaded most, only because it made him appear guilty when he wasn't. "I tried to explain what had happened, but no one listened."

"Wait. Who was there?"

"The company pay clerk, who'd come to check on the delay, and the sheriff's deputy. I could tell they didn't believe me. The deputy sent the pay clerk back to get the mine boss. I knew I'd hang if I stayed. So I drew again, grabbed the deputy's horse, and got away. By the time they got other men out on horses after me, I was too far gone."

"And you came here?"

"Eventually. I spent a few weeks hiding nearby, long enough to know the sheriff had died and the money had disappeared. Long enough to know someone put the blame on me for stealing it." He studied the fine grains in the table. It reminded him of the little table that sat by the door to the room he shared with his father as a child. The table had been his mother's. She'd left it behind—along with everything else—when she'd gone. It was the only thing of hers his father kept, besides a photograph he'd given to Thomas. Why that table, he'd never know. "I lost everything that day. My job, my freedom, my good name. I even lost my father's ring that same day, as we were unloading the company's money into a lockbox."

"I'm sorry," Caroline said, her voice quiet.

"He died when I was seventeen. It was the only thing I had that was his. It was gold, and he wore it on his little finger." He held up his hand as if he could see the ghost of the ring there. Saying these words out loud revived the pain anew. "He raised me alone."

"That couldn't have been an easy task. I'm sorry you lost your mother so young."

Thomas snorted. "Thank you, but she's not dead. Not so far as I know, anyhow."

Caroline's delicate face contorted into confusion.

"She left us." No need to tell her the whole, messy story.

"That's terrible," she said. There was so much emotion behind those two words, one might think it had happened to her instead. "I can't imagine a woman leaving her child."

"It was a long time ago. I don't remember her much." He tried to brush it off, but the way she looked at him . . . It wasn't pity. He couldn't stand pity. It was something else. Something kinder, more empathetic. Almost as if she felt the pain he'd lived through as a child.

She reached out and—ever so briefly—laid a hand on his arm. It was the tiniest gesture of comfort, and it caught him entirely by surprise. Her hand was small and the warmth of it burned through his shirt sleeve. For the briefest moment, he imagined himself a customer in the hotel dining room, having Caroline all to himself as he ordered food for the both of them.

The second she pulled her hand away, he shook his head just slightly to rid it of the ridiculous fantasy.

"I must go," Caroline said, standing up. She looked a bit flustered, and something about that endeared her to him a little more. Women with all the money in the world didn't embarrass easily. But then again, she'd defied that mold more than once already. And that only made him even more curious about her.

"I'm sorry to have kept you." He offered her an elbow, which, to his delight, she took, even though they had only a few feet to walk before they needed to break apart.

"Please don't be." She tilted her face up and looked him in the eyes.

His breath caught. The smile she gave him was genuine, as if she enjoyed spending time in his company. It lit up her face and made her even more beautiful. The few freckles that dotted her cheeks reminded him she was more than just a delicate girl. She was a woman who knew the value of hard work, and that made her all the more appealing. He lifted his other hand, and tucked a piece of her flyaway hair behind her ear. He let his hand linger, wanting more than anything to trace the line of her jaw and brush his fingers over her lips.

She stood perfectly still. Her eyes closed, and then, a moment later, they flew open again. He dropped his hand from where it rested near her ear but held her gaze until she looked away.

"I'll think about your story," she said, her breath a bit ragged. "Perhaps together we can come up with some way to prove your innocence."

He smiled as he let her arm go. She gripped the doorknob like a sailor leaving a ship for the first time in months. He hoped it was because of him. "Thank you," was all he said.

She bestowed a quick, uncertain smile upon him. And then she was gone.

Chapter Fourteen

Caroline awoke to the sounds of Penny moving about their room. She relished the comfort of her bed before stretching and sitting up. The window in their room faced north, and judging from the amount of sunlight filtering through, the morning was half over.

"Hello, sleepyhead," Penny said brightly from where she stood at the washbasin.

"I doubt you've been awake much longer," Caroline said. She yawned. It wouldn't hurt if she lay back down for just a few moments, would it?

Penny laughed as she splashed water on her face. "We'll have to scrounge scraps from the kitchen for breakfast."

Caroline gave in and slid back between the bedclothes. They were so deliciously soft. Her eyes began to close.

"Caroline Beauchamp!" Penny's sharp Southern accent made Caroline's eyelids fly open. "Never in my days have I seen the morning where you weren't leaping out of bed, ready to take on even the hardest task."

"Mmm." The sound came out of Caroline's mouth as her eyes shut again.

A weight pressed on the bed. Caroline slid one eye open to see Penny perched there, staring at her. "May I help you?" she asked sleepily.

"Yes. I'd like to know what kept you up an hour later last night. I may have been asleep when you first returned, but only the dead could sleep through the squeak in that wardrobe door. Did Mrs. Ruby tell you the story of her childhood spent in Prague when you returned downstairs?"

"Mrs. Ruby is from Indiana," Caroline said, fighting to keep her eyes open.

Penny poked her shoulder. "I *know* that. But what I don't know is what kept you out so late. And don't think I'm leaving you be until you tell me."

Caroline pushed herself into a seated position, yawning. She'd been wanting to tell Penny everything, but she couldn't betray Thomas's trust. Not to mention, she knew how much Penny loved gossip. Perhaps a tiny bit of the truth would suffice. "I was speaking with a man."

The incredulous look Penny gave her nearly made Caroline wish she could've lied. A falsehood would've sounded more believable that what she'd just said.

"Caroline Beauchamp." Penny pronounced her full name, emphasizing every syllable, for the second time that morning. "I wouldn't have been more surprised if you'd said you'd gone for a midnight ride to the mining camp."

Caroline stifled a laugh. That was highly improbable, and Penny knew it. Thanks to taking a spill off a horse when she was seven years old, Caroline had retained quite the fear of riding. And stepping foot into the wild mining encampment a few miles to the east was not something she ever wished to do. "It's true," she said.

"Well, I need more details than that. Who is he? What's his name? Is he handsome? Do I know him? How did you meet him?"

Caroline giggled like a child. "First, I must swear you to secrecy. If anyone finds out, I could lose my position."

Penny nodded. "You do know I was the first person Emma told about her Mr. Hartley? I kept her secret for weeks. I would've kept it forever, if she'd needed me to."

Caroline blinked in surprise. She'd planned to give vague answers to Penny's questions in order to keep Thomas's identity hidden. But perhaps Penny was better at keeping secrets than Caroline had realized.

As if she'd read Caroline's mind, Penny said, "When it comes to the truly important things, I'm like a safe in the bank." She undid her long braid as she said this, and now she finger-combed her golden brown curls as she waited for Caroline to speak.

"Well . . ." Caroline trailed off, trying to figure out where to begin. "His name is Thomas. He's tall and . . ." She blushed as she thought of his ocean-colored eyes on her, his sun-lightened hair curling over his collar, the warmth of his hand on her wrist. "Nice. He's very nice."

"Nice?" Penny fixed her with an indignant look. "I was hoping for something more like dashing, or dangerous, or rich—" She was cut off as Caroline tossed a pillow at her face. She laughed and slung it back at Caroline, who caught it and dissolved into giggles herself.

"All right! Please, though, do me one favor," Penny said when she caught her breath. "Be discreet."

They were quiet for a moment. Caroline knew exactly what Penny meant. Emma had been dismissed over just such a situation.

"I will. Besides, it's nothing like that. I'm simply helping him with a problem he has." Caroline flattened her pillow behind her, but even out of the corner of her eye, she could see Penny raise her eyebrows. A part of her heart ached in an unfamiliar way, as if she wished there was something more to her conversations with Thomas. Heat crept up her neck as she remembered the way he'd touched her face last night. Why had he done such a thing? More importantly, why had she let him? She shouldn't have, and not just because she wanted to keep her job. "And anyhow, I want to keep working as a Gilbert Girl. I'm going to be named head waitress."

Penny grinned. "And to think that when we arrived here, I was certain you'd be on a train home by midsummer." She paused. "You'll get the title. Dora, Millie, and I will do everything we can to help you."

Caroline flushed with warmth. She was so grateful to have made friends such as these. Penny quickly dressed and pinned up her hair, claiming she was famished. Caroline took her time. In truth, she wanted a few moments to herself to parse out her thoughts.

After Penny left, Caroline sat at the small dressing table, brushing her long hair. It glowed in the sunlight from the window, gold and white-blonde. Her mother had told her such a shade of hair was a blessing, and she should use it to her advantage. The advice nearly made Caroline laugh out loud now. All the practice she'd had at attracting men, all the advice about acting just coquettish enough to draw their attention, but not so much as to make them think her ill-bred—all of it was for naught. What was the point of sending a man a small smile over the top of a fan when her father had already chosen the man she would marry?

And that man was nothing like the man she'd imagined marrying. He was much older, gruff, balding, and had a pot belly. But it wasn't his looks so much as his demeanor—and the rumors that followed him—that had terrified Caroline into fleeing the only home she'd ever known. Her mind flitted back to the creek yesterday, when Thomas had found her and held her as she cried. He hadn't laughed, hadn't pried or told her she was acting ridiculous. He'd been tender and caring. And when he spoke of his family last night . . . Losing both of his parents, even if his mother was still alive somewhere, had left him scarred somewhere deep inside. She could see that much just in his eyes. He was a different person than she'd assumed he was when she'd first met him. And when he'd brushed her face with his hand while tucking that piece of hair behind her ear . . .

She wound her hair into a chignon and pinned it into place. Instead of thinking about how kind he'd been or how hurt he was or—even worse—his hand on her face, she needed to focus on helping him prove his innocence. And to do that, she needed to speak with him again.

Chapter Fifteen

Thomas set the hammer down. He'd spent the day repairing the hinges on the door to the smithy shop, then nailing shingles to its roof, and now he was building more shelving. He'd never built so many shelves in his life as he had in the past few days. He'd set up his work behind the smithy rather than his previous spot behind the hotel to make it easier to install the finished products.

The smithy clanged away on a set of horseshoes as Thomas studied the shelf he'd just finished. He was improving, at least. Working on the hotel all summer had given him a set of skills he'd never possessed, and now, working on even finer pieces, he was honing those skills. He wasn't sure he wanted to be a carpenter, but for now, he was grateful for whatever work he could do to survive and stay hidden.

"Thomas." His name was a whisper on the cool wind that blew down from the Sangre de Cristo Mountains at his back.

He looked up, and there, standing behind the smithy shop, was Caroline. She wore her usual gray and white garb, her sunshine-colored hair pinned up behind the matching hat. It was a warm enough afternoon to go without a coat. Her face was pink from the wind, and her smile . . . It could cheer up even the grumpiest of men. She was happy to see him, and that small fact alone made Thomas feel as giddy as if he'd just slung back a shot of whiskey.

He glanced around. No one was nearby except the smithy inside his shop. This side of the tracks was largely abandoned now that the hotel was open. But still, they could be none too careful. He pointed to the large white house that sat several yards away. It had been where the first Gilbert Girls stayed while the hotel was built, but it stood empty now.

Caroline retreated across the grass and sage. He waited a few moments before setting down the shelf he was pretending to examine and joining her.

She was leaning back against the rear wall of the house. "I'm sorry to interrupt your work. I'm between trains, and I hoped I could steal a few moments to ask you some questions."

He raised his eyebrows as he leaned a hand against the building. "Aren't you afraid I'll think you too forward?"

"About your . . . incident. Not about you. You think much too highly of yourself, Mr. Drexel."

"Oh, are we back to formalities? In that case, I'll have to say I'm quite disappointed, Miss Beauchamp. Here I'd thought you pulled me away from my duties to find out my favorite food, or ask me my favorite scent." Her cheeks went even pinker, and he couldn't help but smile.

"On the contrary, I prefer to keep my position here. I'm well on my way to head waitress." She drew her shoulders back and lifted her chin.

"That's quite impressive." It reminded him of that day by the creek, when she'd told him her job meant everything to her. He'd assumed she'd meant that she needed to keep her position for practical reasons, and he knew she worked hard to do so. But she looked so proud right now, after telling him about her chances for moving up. All he could do was stand there and blink at her, like a man rendered mute. True love for her work wasn't something he'd imagined mattered to a woman with a background like Caroline's. According to his father, his own mother was appalled at the idea of taking in laundry or mending to help earn money. Caroline must have been raised similarly, letting others do everything for her. It made no sense—nothing about her did—and suddenly, he needed to know. "How did you come to be here?"

She laughed. "I answered an ad, the same as every other girl here." She continued to smile at him, and he almost forgot his name. Her smile was all-consuming, as if no other woman had ever smiled before.

He finally dragged his eyes away from her lips and glanced at the bent grasses below his feet in order to pull his thoughts together again. "I meant you specifically. You strike me as a woman who comes from a well-to-do family. You told me you didn't wish for anyone to know you're here. How did you ever find yourself in this place?" Her smile faltered, and he wondered if he'd pushed too far. "Forgive me, I've asked too much."

"No." She clasped her hands in front of her and closed her eyes for a moment. "I mean, you have. But it's nothing the girls don't already know." When she looked up at him, her sky-colored eyes were watery, as if she were holding back tears again. He wanted to reach out, take her in his arms once more, and tell her nothing would hurt her here.

Get a hold of yourself, Drexel. Those kinds of thoughts would lead to nothing but trouble. The last thing he needed was to end up like his father, working his fingers to the bone for an ungrateful woman. Except . . . each time he spoke with her, Caroline seemed less and less like a spoiled rich girl and more like someone who valued hard work.

"My family is well-known in Boston society. We—they—own a shipping and import company that my grandfather founded. I have a brother, Quentin, who will inherit it all. I was expected to marry well." She looked away for a moment, searching across the valley toward the dark Wet Mountains to the east, as if she'd find resolve buried somewhere in the pine trees that dotted the landscape or the small hills that rose before the mountains. She turned back to him, her eyes meeting his own. "My father chose someone for me. I . . . didn't care for him. So I left."

"You gave up your entire life and your family because you didn't care for the man your father wanted you to marry?"

She shook her head. "It wasn't that simple. I'd been led to believe I could choose my own husband. But I wasn't given a choice. I . . " She pressed her lips together. "I'm much better off here."

"Surely there were other avenues you could have taken instead?" Thomas asked, although he couldn't blame her for running in such a situation.

She crossed her arms. "None that would've let me disappear so thoroughly. I know what you're thinking. How could a pampered, society-minded girl who'd never done anything more difficult than needlepoint adapt to hard work in an environment such as this?"

He could've laughed, if it had been appropriate. "That's exactly what I'm thinking."

She tilted her chin up and a proud smile crossed her face. "I'm much stronger than I look, even if I didn't believe it myself when I arrived here. I thought of giving up so many times last summer, but I didn't. I kept trying, and I succeeded. And now here I am, very close to convincing Mrs. Ruby that I deserve to be head waitress."

She looked at him with such fierce pride, it could've knocked him down. It made him want to know everything about Caroline Beauchamp, as dangerous as it was to both their positions. And somehow—maybe by the way she watched him or the way she continued to seek him out—he thought she might feel the same way.

"How about you, Thomas?" she asked.

He was certain he'd never tire of hearing her say his name. "What do you mean?"

"What do you want? I wanted the ability to make my own decisions. And now I do."

He slid his hand off the wooden siding and into his pocket. What did he want? He hadn't asked himself that question in a long time. "Right now? Freedom."

"And after that?"

"I'm not certain."

She kept staring at him, the shadow from the house covering her face and making those tiny freckles disappear into the rest of her skin. He wanted to reach up and trace them so badly he had to clench his hands in his pockets to keep them in place. His fingers burned with the memory of brushing against her cheek last night. He didn't know what had possessed him. At least he hadn't scared her off.

"Surely there's something you wanted from life before you had to go on the run," she pressed.

There was, but he hadn't thought about it in months. Not when his primary concern was simply staying alive. "I'd like to run my own business. A mercantile, perhaps. It's . . . something my father always wanted, but never had."

Her smile was blinding. "That's wonderful!"

Her enthusiasm caught him off-guard. He faltered a second before returning her smile. He decided he wouldn't quite mind standing here, behind this old house in the long afternoon shadows, forever.

A shout from across the tracks made them both start.

"It's McFarland," he said. "I'd better return to my work."

"Oh! But I didn't ask you what I'd intended." Caroline smoothed her dress and straightened her hat, never mind that neither had gathered a single wrinkle from simply standing in one place.

"Then you'll have to find me again later." He doffed an imaginary hat at her, his real one having been left behind the smithy's, and shot her a rakish grin before turning his back and striding across the broken grass.

When he glanced back, she was watching him. And this made him happier than he could have ever imagined.

Chapter Sixteen

"That man's sermons are still remarkably dull." Penny clasped a hand to her old scarlet hat as the wind kicked up.

"I thought it was informative," Caroline said as she picked her way around mud that had accumulated on the wooden planks that lined the sides of the street in Cañon City. "Just because he tempers his voice and chooses to avoid speaking on hellfire doesn't mean the sermon is dull."

"If you say so." Penny's attention had shifted to the windows of a dry goods store.

Caroline paused as her friend examined the fabrics and ribbons on display in the large window. The sermon had been awfully long, but they still had a few hours to spend in Cañon City before Mr. and Mrs. McFarland would expect them and the other girls who'd had this overcast Sunday off back at the livery to return home. Since the train only ran twice a day—once in each direction—they were still dependent on buckboards if they wanted to attend services.

"Do you want to go in?" Caroline asked Penny.

Penny sighed, her breath fogging the glass. "No. I need to send all my earnings home this month. Mama wrote and told me she'd been ill and hasn't been able to work for a couple of weeks."

"I'm sorry. I hope she's feeling better."

Penny smiled through the far-off look in her eyes, the one she always got when speaking of her mother. "But I am willing to part with some of it for dinner." She pointed to a small establishment across the muddy street.

"Mrs. Smith's Home Cooking," Caroline read from the sign affixed to the front of the building. While most of the shops and businesses along the street were nondescript, Mrs. Smith had painted her restaurant in a cheerful yellow. It looked like a welcoming sort of place.

The girls stepped carefully across the street, dodging horses and wagons and trying in vain not to step in dung or muddy their shoes too badly. Inside, the single room was simply decorated, but comfortable and inviting. A tiny spray of flowers sat in a glass jar on each wooden table, and a rose-patterned paper covered the walls. The room was full, but Caroline and Penny found one last empty table.

A girl no older than sixteen arrived to greet them and take their orders, while a boy who looked just like her peeked out from the kitchen.

"It's nice to be the one sitting at the table for a change," Penny said.

"It certainly is." Caroline relaxed into her chair and enjoyed simply being off her feet at a mealtime.

They were nearly finished with plates of pot roast, carrots, and fluffy potatoes when the front door to the restaurant burst open. A man lurched inside, his hat askew. He was several steps into the restaurant before he seemed to realize he should remove it from his head. He stopped near Caroline and Penny as he searched the room for an empty table, of which there were none to be had.

"Pardon me, ladies," he said, his breath ripe with drink. "There don't seem to be any free tables. How's about I join you for dinner?" He promptly sat in one of the free chairs at their table and leaned forward on his elbows.

Caroline recoiled. She was about to tell him he was quite unwelcome when Penny spoke first.

"Sir, you are drunk, and you need to remove yourself from our table." Penny's voice was firm but quiet.

"That's not very neighborly of you, Miss . . ." His eyes roved over Penny. Penny stiffened. "I'm gonna call you Lillian. 'Cause you look like a Lillian. And you . . ." His gaze swung to Caroline and lingered there as it turned into a leer.

It made her stomach feel as if it was about to lose all the good food she'd just eaten. "You need to leave, immediately. Before we need to call for assistance."

"Clara," he declared. "That's what I'm gonna call you. Now, Lillian, Clara, which of you ladies might like to accompany me back to the saloon?"

Caroline gasped. How dare he imply they were so improper? Her entire body went hot, and before she knew what she was doing, she'd stood, lifted her hand, and smacked the man hard across the face.

Penny stared at her in shock before a smile lifted her lips. Caroline's eyes dropped to her hand, which was shaking. When she looked up, the man was also standing, his hard-lined face ruddy with more than just drink. He reached out and clumsily grabbed her arm, his fingers digging into her through the fabric of her sleeve.

"Now I like 'em feisty, Clara, but that's about gone too far."

Caroline pulled away, but he held tight. "Let me go." Her voice betrayed her, shaky instead of sounding firm.

"You need to learn some manners, missy," he said.

"No, you'd better unhand her before I hit you so hard, you'll think you see Heaven itself." Penny stood, her hands on her hips. "And don't think I can't do it. I've hit plenty of men before."

The man laughed, a guffaw that silenced the restaurant patrons who weren't already watching them. "Maybe you should both come with me then. I do like the girls who cause trouble."

"Let the lady go," a male voice said from across the table.

Caroline turned. There, standing opposite the drunk man, was a tall, broad-shouldered man. He was neatly dressed, and a metal star sat perched on his gray jacket.

"Lawman," the drunk fellow said unnecessarily. "I ain't doing anything. Just having a conversation with these here girls."

"Conversations don't generally involve ladies hitting gentlemen," the tall man said, his deep voice steady and with an undercurrent of danger. "Unhand her or I'll help you find the sheriff here. I'm on my way there myself, so it wouldn't be any extra burden."

The man's grip slackened before his hand fell away completely. He said nothing as he lumbered to the door and out of the restaurant.

"Thank you," Caroline said, smoothing her skirt to hide the nerves that still made her hands tremble.

"Yes, thank you, although we were perfectly able to handle him ourselves," Penny added, although Caroline detected just a hint of wobble in her voice.

"You're welcome. I don't take kindly to ladies being harassed. Now I wonder if you couldn't do me a favor—I've only just arrived in town—and tell me where the county sheriff's office is?"

"I wish we could," Caroline said, "but we're only visiting Cañon City." She sat, her legs feeling as if she'd just gotten off a cross-country train ride.

"I apologize. I assumed you were residents of this fine town." The sheriff tapped his hat against his thigh as he glanced around the restaurant, presumably looking for other men he could boot from the establishment before turning his gaze back on Penny and Caroline. "Are you here long?"

"Only for the day. We're employed with the Gilbert Company in Crest Stone." Penny's chin lifted with pride.

"Ah, I see. A fine company. I may end up down that way if I don't find who I'm after here."

Penny's eyes widened. "Are you searching for an outlaw?"

"Indeed. The man who murdered my predecessor. He's known as Tom the Cat."

Caroline's heart nearly lurched to a stop.

The man was after Thomas.

Chapter Seventeen

The moon rode high in a sky pricked with stars as Thomas waited with a horse for Caroline. She'd found him in the kitchens as he stood, scarfing down a bowl of beef stew. Her eyes darting around the room, she told him she needed to speak with him alone as soon as possible. He didn't ask her why, although he hoped it was because she had an idea that hadn't yet occurred to him about how to prove his innocence. Although, if he were being honest, the way his heart lifted at her request had nothing to do with his past problems and everything to do with spending more time in Caroline's presence. He'd suggested meeting outside, late, and now here he was.

As the minutes ticked by, he feared she'd changed her mind. She'd told him that the Gilbert Girls were expected to be in their rooms by ten o'clock each night. And then, of course, there was the not so small fact that she wasn't supposed to be spending time with him at all, and especially not alone. He was asking a lot of her to meet him out here.

Thomas sighed and checked his pocket watch with his free hand. It was ten minutes past eleven. Perhaps she wasn't coming. She'd either come to her senses and decided to leave well enough alone with him, or she'd been prevented from leaving in some way. He hoped it was the latter. He clucked to the horse, and just as they'd taken a step forward, Caroline emerged from around the corner of the hotel. Thomas caught his breath. She looked like an angel with the moonlight making her hair shine a white gold. Her simple cream calico dress almost glowed.

"Is this your horse?" she asked. "He's beautiful." She ran a hand down the horse's red-brown neck, and he nickered in return.

"I wish, but he belongs to the company. Do you ride?"

She made a face, then laughed. "Terribly. To be honest, I'm a bit nervous on horseback. I took a fall as a child, and I fear I've never recovered from it."

"This shouldn't be quite so exciting. All you have to do is hold on. I'll take care of the horse."

"Hold on?" She glanced at the horse, then at him. Her eyes widened as if she'd just figured out what he meant. "I can't . . . I mean, we shouldn't . . . It really isn't proper . . ."

Thomas laughed. Her loss for words was endearing. "You try so hard to hold on to what you were taught is acceptable, even though you left that life far behind you."

She straightened and put her hands on her hips. "Part of the Gilbert Girls' work here is to bring civilization to a wild place."

"And you are. But out here . . ." He opened one arm wide as he held the horse's reins with the other. "Some of those old rules no longer apply. You need to relax a little."

"Are you implying I'm too prim?" If she could draw herself up any taller, she'd maybe meet his chin.

He grinned. "No . . . not particularly."

One hand dropped from her hips, and for a moment, he thought she'd swat him. He almost wished she would. It would be good for her.

"All I'm saying is that this is nothing more than a horseback ride to a place we can sit and converse without worrying about who will overhear."

"A horseback ride *together*," she corrected him.

"If you prefer, I can ride and you can walk alongside me." He laughed when her mouth fell open, then decided to try another tack. "I dare you, Miss Caroline Beauchamp, to get on this horse with me."

She pressed her lips together. "Fine. But if anything untoward—"

"For the love of all creation, just get on the horse!"

She stepped forward and placed one hand on the saddle. "I . . . oh!"

Thomas had placed both hands on her waist to lift her up. He ignored the little voice in the back of his head that wanted him to pull her to him. Instead, he lifted her just high enough that she could reach the saddle.

Caroline arranged herself so she sat sideways on the saddle facing Thomas.

He lifted his hat to push his hair back from his face. "Honey, you can't sit like that. There's no room for me."

Her face blanched. "What did you just call me?"

What did he call her? *Honey*. He could've kicked himself. "I'm sorry," he said. "Are you going to sit up there the right way or not?"

"I can't sit astride." Her face had contorted into a look of absolute horror.

It was enough to make him forget his indiscretion as the smile fought its way across his lips. "If you sit up near the front, you can wrap a leg around the horn. It's not the same, but it's as close as you're going to get." When she didn't move, he added, "Remember where you are?"

She closed her eyes a second. "The old rules don't apply." Her words were so quiet, it was almost as if she were speaking to herself. She drew a deep breath, grabbed hold of the saddle horn to pull herself forward, and then slung one leg around it. No matter how she arranged them, her skirts didn't quite cover her ankles. Thomas knew the immodesty had to be eating her up inside. "Satisfied?" she asked, her face pink in the moonlight.

Her irritation at something so trite made him grin. "I am, thank you." He pulled himself up to sit behind her.

She gasped as he slid his arms around her to take the reins. Having her this close to him was unnerving. She was so warm and small in his arms, and it immediately made him think of that afternoon by the creek when he'd held her as she cried.

He took a few deep breaths. He'd never make it to the spot he'd picked out if he couldn't get his mind off her mere *closeness*.

He clucked to the horse, and they headed south. A tremble shuddered through her body, so small he almost didn't notice. Then there was another one. And another.

She was frightened.

Of course. He could've smacked himself for forgetting. "You're safe, I promise. It's awfully hard to fall off a horse going this slow, especially when you've got me right here."

She sighed so quietly, he wouldn't have heard her if the night hadn't been so still. But slowly, she relaxed. The trembling stopped, her shoulders dropped, and she even let her back give in until she was braced against his chest. At least until she realized what she'd done and straightened back up again.

He veered to the left about a mile in, and there it was behind two lone cottonwood trees—a tiny, one-room log cabin.

"Who lives here?" Caroline asked as he reined up the horse just outside of it.

"No one. It's abandoned. Someone tried to make a go of ranching here several years ago. They likely moved north, where the other ranches are." He slid off and held out his hands to help her. She clasped them, and he tried not to think about how small they felt in his own.

Once on the ground, she let go and straightened her skirts before looking back up at the little cabin, her eyes taking the whole thing in. "It's adorable."

His heart lifted as he tied the horse to one of the posts on the front porch. He'd hoped she would like it, but had also been prepared for her to be horrified at its size or its remoteness, or the fact that no one had lived in it for years.

"But what are we doing here?" She lifted her face to look at him.

"We're borrowing the place." He reached for the saddlebags. "For a small picnic."

Caroline's face broke into a smile, and a jolt of glee flooded Thomas. He'd do anything to have her smile at him. Something about it lit him up inside in a way he hadn't felt since his father had been alive.

"Shall we sit on the porch?" she asked.

"You'll be pleased to know I already have us set up inside, at a proper table." He crooked his elbow as if he were a gentleman at one of those balls she was likely used to back East. "May I escort you to your seat?"

She chewed her lip as she hung back on the lowest step to the porch. "We'd be alone inside, and—"

"It's not appropriate?" He tilted his head and gave her his best innocent grin. "I believe we've already established that you need to do away with your high societal standards. It's nearly midnight, and no one is awake but us and the coyotes. Your reputation is safe. If you trust me, that is. Do you trust me?"

She blinked at him, her pretty face set into thought. A moment went by where all Thomas could hear was the beating of his own heart, the chill wind raking through the cottonwoods, and, as if to remind them what Thomas had said was true, the distant howl of a coyote.

"I trust you," Caroline finally said.

Thomas had never wanted to hear three words more than those. As Caroline closed the few steps between them and slid her arm into his, he thought his heart might burst.

He had never been happier than he was in this moment.

"Our picnic awaits," he said as he led her into the cabin.

Chapter Eighteen

Caroline was fairly certain her mouth was hanging open in a most unladylike manner when Thomas lit a lamp inside the old cabin. He had spared no detail. He'd covered the small table in a white cloth that looked suspiciously like the ones in the Crest Stone Hotel Restaurant. Two silver candleholders held white candles, which Thomas lit as Caroline stood back by the door. He'd set the table in china that was *exactly* the sort that sat upon the restaurant's tables.

"I know what you're thinking. Have no fear, I'll return it all clean and in one piece. No one will ever know it was missing." He extinguished the lit match and pulled out one of the chairs for her.

"Thank you," she said. He pushed the chair in as she sat. "This really is lovely. Where did you find the flowers?" The valley had been bereft of flowers since the first frost.

"They're dried. One of the maids enjoys making those little silk bags with dried flower petals."

"Sachets?" Caroline said.

"That's it. She gave me a few of her finds."

Caroline tried to contain her surprise. He'd put a lot of effort into this. The light was dim, but she was almost certain he'd even swept the floor and dusted the other surfaces around them. It was going to be difficult enough already to tell him what had happened in Cañon City, and now she hated to ruin the evening by sharing such dour news.

He bowed, the saddlebag still slung over his arm. "For dinner tonight, miss, we have bread, a selection of cheeses, sliced ham, and fine aged water. Shall I pour you a glass?"

She giggled, and from nowhere, he produced a pitcher of water and poured the liquid into her glass. "Thank you, sir."

From the saddlebag, he pulled out brown paper packages filled with the food of which he'd spoken and placed some on each of their plates. Caroline waited until he was seated before she picked up a knife to slice a piece of bread. But the knife remained suspended above her food as Thomas lifted his hunk of bread and proceeded to tear a piece off with his teeth. He then rolled up a slice of meat on his fork and took a large bite of it.

"What?" he asked once he'd swallowed.

Caroline finally put her knife down. She wasn't certain how to broach the subject without hurting his feelings. He'd told her his mother had left when he was young, and it was clear his father had never taken the time to teach him proper table manners.

She drew in a breath and clasped her hands in her lap under the table. An idea blossomed, and she plunged ahead with it. "Do you remember how you told me you wished to own a business?"

He nodded and slurped some water.

Caroline pushed her lips together, cringing. "If you did, you'd be a businessman, a pillar of some town or another. Respected by other townsfolk and meeting regularly with other men of similar societal rank."

Thomas smiled, as if the idea pleased him, and then laughed. "I'm sure they'd see right through me."

"Nonsense." Caroline raised her knife again as she spoke and began slicing a bite-sized piece of bread onto her plate. "All you have to do is act like them. Anyone could learn. Then, as far as they'd know, your background would be no different from theirs."

Thomas watched her slice off a bit of cheese, place it on the bread, and then spear both bread and cheese with a fork.

"I could . . . teach you. If you'd like."

He scratched at the stubble on his face, as if he were thinking about it.

"It's simple, really." Caroline looked up at him through her lashes. "After all, you're teaching me how to lose some of my insistence on what's proper. Why shouldn't I help you learn what I know?"

"All right, then. Teach me to eat like the wealthy."

She almost couldn't believe he agreed. "First lesson. Cut your food into pieces, one at a time." She demonstrated again, and he followed suit. "Lesson two, never use your hands. Always use a fork."

"What if I'm having soup?" He gave her a crooked smile.

She laughed. "Then of course you use a spoon. Next time, we'll go over the use of each utensil."

"Next time?"

Her face went warm, and she turned all of her attention to her food. She didn't know where that had come from. Perhaps his lessons were sinking in. He watched her as she cut a piece of ham. When she looked up, his eyes were still on her.

"You look lovely tonight."

An even warmer blush rose to her cheeks. And here she thought she looked a mess, her hair hastily put up in the dark and wearing the simplest dress she owned. She'd had to sneak out of the room she shared with Penny. "Thank you," she finally said, her eyes still on her plate. When she looked up again, he was still watching her. His eyes were a dark gray in the candlelight. She marveled at how they seemed to change colors from day to day. But now . . . they seemed to darken even more as he looked at her.

His jaw worked, almost as if he wanted to say something. She remained quiet, waiting for him. Finally, he spoke. "I wanted to thank you for trusting me. Not just here, tonight. But since the day you found out about what happened at Barrett Mountain. You've believed in me, which is far more than I ever expected anyone to do."

"Of course I do." Caroline's hands fell to the napkin in her lap. "You've done nothing but be honest with me. How could I not want to help you?"

He watched her so intently, no hint of teasing or joking to hide his pain, that it almost split her heart in two. "You're the only one."

She twisted the napkin in her hands. She had to tell him about Cañon City. It was his life on the line, and he deserved to know someone was looking for him. "Something happened when I went into town on Sunday."

"Oh?" Thomas sat back in his chair, his plate now empty.

"Penny and I were having dinner in a little restaurant when a drunken man accosted us."

Thomas sat forward, his face going dark. "Accosted you? What did he do, exactly?"

She swallowed. Even thinking about that horrible man's hand wrapped around her wrist made her feel sick. "He was under the impression that we were . . . well . . . not well-bred ladies. He grabbed hold of me—"

Thomas stood up and began pacing. "Did he do anything else? I promise you he'll regret it."

Caroline shook her head, although her heart warmed at his protectiveness. "There's no need for that. Another man—a sheriff from some other town—came to our rescue and dispatched him right away. That is, after I slapped the drunkard."

He finally stopped pacing, but he didn't sit. "If he ever bothers you again, I want you to tell me immediately."

"I will, but only if you promise not to act brashly."

"I can't promise such a thing." He stood there, his face in shadows, and she knew he was telling the truth. Caroline prayed she'd never see that man again. The last thing Thomas needed was another burden on his soul. His face relaxed a little. "Did you really slap him?"

"I did." Caroline lifted her chin. She wanted to revel in the look of pride he gave her, but there was something else Thomas needed to know. She pushed her chair back and stood too. Perhaps this would be easier if she was on her feet. She placed a hand on the back of her chair and looked Thomas in the eye. "The sheriff who came to our rescue mentioned he was looking for Tom the Cat."

Chapter Nineteen

Thomas stood rooted to the cabin's wooden floor. It couldn't be.

"He doesn't know you're here," Caroline said. She still held on to the back of that chair like it gave her the strength to tell him such news. "I don't know if he's following a lead or if he's simply moving from town to town. He was on his way to speak with the sheriff in Cañon City."

"What did he look like?" Thomas finally said.

"He was tall and broad. Short hair that was something of a rusty color. He was quite imposing."

Deputy Frank Rayburn. Sheriff now, he supposed. And not elected, as sheriffs should be. The mining company hired him directly to keep order in Barrett Mountain. They simply borrowed the title to make him look legitimate. He'd had no beef with Rayburn as a deputy. In fact, he'd never had trouble with Sheriff Ratterman either, until Ratterman had attempted to steal the entire town's pay from him.

"Do you know him?" Caroline asked tentatively. She'd stepped away from the chair and was now standing before him, her small hands clasped tightly together in front of her.

"I do. He was the deputy in the mining town. Barrett Mountain."

"The one who came with the pay clerk the day the sheriff tried to steal the money?"

"The very one."

"What should we do now?"

"We?" He laughed, and then immediately wished he hadn't when he saw the wounded look that crossed her face. He reached for her hand, allowing himself to make the contact he'd been wanting to all night. When she didn't protest, he took both her hands in his and looked down into her face. "I'm sorry. I didn't mean to be cruel. I just don't want you hurt."

"How would I get hurt? All I want to do is help you prove your innocence." Her hands shifted in his as she took a hesitant step forward.

He kept his eyes on her face, trying not to think about how close she was to him for the second time that night. He could barely think at all as they'd ridden down here, her small body cocooned in his on the saddle. He closed his eyes for a second to keep his focus. And in that moment, he never wanted to run again. Not if it hurt her, because if there was anything he wanted even more than his own freedom, it was to make this woman happy. But how could he do that as a wanted man? Especially now that the man who was searching for him was so nearby? A frustrated sigh escaped his lips.

"I still believe we can prove to this sheriff that you were defending yourself and the company's money." Caroline looked up at him with all the hope in the world in her eyes.

"But that's the problem. I've been around this so many times, and I can't think of anything. And before you suggest it, yes, I have thought that Rayburn was the one who stole the money. And the pay clerk, too. But neither of those is possible."

"How come?" Caroline asked. She'd had the same thoughts. After all, it seemed obvious from the facts of Thomas's story.

"Rayburn had no horse because I'd taken it. He had no way to transport that lockbox without taking the entire wagon, which would have looked very suspicious. He had no friends who would help him. Rayburn was not particularly liked in the camp. And the clerk was a nervous man. He couldn't even skip Sunday services without everyone knowing, simply because of the anxious countenance that would sit on his face the whole week."

"How about witnesses?" Caroline asked. "Did anyone else see what happened?"

He shook his head. The girl was determined, he had to give her that. "No one arrived until after the shooting."

"Do you know for certain?"

"Yes . . ." He trailed off. *Did* he know for certain? The events of that evening had such sharp focus, but he'd never looked beyond what had been right in front of him. "I think so. But I suppose there could have been someone I never saw."

She chewed her lip as she looked at him. "How about clues? Was there anything left at the crossroads?"

He hadn't even thought of that. "I don't think so." He dropped one of her hands to rub at his face. "If there was anything there, I didn't see it."

"But you didn't have time to look either, did you?"

"No. I didn't." He couldn't think of anything that *could* have been there. Any tracks left in the dirt would be long gone by now. Any coins dropped would have been picked up as miners walked from town to mine.

She smiled victoriously. "See, there are possibilities. You only have to think on it some more, and I just know something will come to you."

She looked so proud of herself that he couldn't help but smile back, even though his future seemed to be nothing but a black curtain. But she had a point. There was a lot he didn't know. And if that was the case, then maybe there was something or someone out there who could prove he was in the right.

"I don't want to see you taken to prison," she said softly as she looked up at him with those beautiful blue eyes.

Seeing her look at him like that, having her say that to him . . . his heart filled. No one had ever believed in him the way she did. He lifted a hand and traced a finger along her cheek. She took a sharp breath and closed her eyes. What he wouldn't give to press her to him right now and kiss her so thoroughly that she'd be his forever.

But he couldn't. He wouldn't scare her away. Somehow, this beautiful, kind woman—who was nothing that he had expected her to be—trusted him, and he wouldn't squander that.

He opened his hand and cupped her cheek, then let go. Her eyes fluttered open and she gave him a look of pure confusion.

"I should get you back to the hotel," he said by way of explanation.

She nodded, but her mouth dropped almost as if she was sad. His heart swelled again. As she blew out the candles, Thomas wondered how he'd gotten so lucky as to meet her in the midst of the chaos of his life. She moved to stack the plates, as if to take them out for washing. In that moment, he couldn't believe he'd ever thought her to be anything like his mother.

"Leave them," he said, his voice a bit garbled. He cleared his throat. "I'll take care of them in the morning."

As he led her out the door to the waiting horse, he fought the one thought that had been drifting around the recesses of his mind since she'd suggested there might be proof out there to exonerate him.

He was going to need to return to Barrett Mountain.

Chapter Twenty

"Mrs. Ruby is going to announce it today!" one of the newer girls said as she flew through the hotel lobby past the other girls filing toward the restaurant before the noon train's arrival.

"Vivian! Decorum, please." Mrs. Ruby's voice called across the lobby.

"Do you suppose it's true?" Caroline whispered to Penny as they entered the dining room. "I thought it would be at least another week before she made a decision."

"We'll find out." Penny squeezed her hand. "But I know you'll get it."

Caroline tried to smile, but nerves prevented her. In fact, she'd become so nervous that she no longer felt tired from her midnight excursion with Thomas.

Thomas. Thankfully she had a healthy dose of anxiety right now, or else thoughts of him caressing her face and riding in the same saddle together would have her far too much of a mess to prove herself worthy of a position here at all, never mind one as head waitress.

"Attention, ladies!"

The chatter ceased instantaneously when Mrs. Ruby spoke. "Thanks to Miss Williamson, I'm sure you all know I've made a decision concerning our head and assistant head waitresses."

Penny gave Caroline a huge smile. Dora and Millie crowded in behind them.

"You've all worked very hard this past week, and I couldn't be prouder of you. That said, we must ensure we never get too comfortable. For if we do, our service will suffer." Mrs. Ruby cast her gaze across the sea of gray-and-white uniformed young ladies before her. She let her words sink in before continuing. "Now for our announcements."

Dora slipped her hand into Caroline's as Caroline sent up a prayer, and then immediately felt guilty. She shouldn't pray for such selfish things.

"Our assistant head waitress is Miss Sarah Taylor."

A squeal arose from the end of the group, and everyone clapped. Millie applauded the loudest. Sarah had arrived in Millie's small group halfway through the summer, and Caroline and her friends had been responsible for training them.

"And our head waitress is Miss Caroline Beauchamp." Mrs. Ruby's proud smile landed on Caroline. "Please come up here, ladies."

Caroline stood rooted to the dining room floor. Mrs. Ruby had chosen her! All of her hard work hadn't gone unnoticed. While, thankfully, her . . . dalliance with Thomas had. Shame crept up the back of her neck. A true Gilbert Girl shouldn't have been acting the way Caroline had. And now that she was head waitress, she *especially* shouldn't be so cavalier about breaking the rules.

"What are you waiting for? Go on." Penny gave her a little nudge in the back.

Even though she stumbled forward, Caroline was thankful for Penny's push. She made her way to Mrs. Ruby on numb feet. Sarah was already there, something small and silver gleaming from the left side of her uniform apron, beneath her collar.

"Miss Beauchamp," Mrs. Ruby said, looking serious again. "I am honored to present you with this pin that indicates your new position." She held out a shining gold star.

Caroline took it gratefully and pinned it to her apron. "Thank you. I'm humbled. And I promise to do my best as head waitress."

Mrs. Ruby beamed. "You are both a shining example of what the Gilbert Company strives to be to the world." She moved her eyes to the girls standing behind Caroline and Sarah. "We are to be beacons of civilization in the wilderness, ever polite, humble, graceful, and willing to serve."

Caroline's face reddened, and she ducked her head, hoping no one saw. She felt like a fraud, standing up here as some kind of example of a Gilbert Girl. Yes, she worked hard and she exceeded Mrs. Ruby's expectations, but in her own hours, she was flaunting all the rules. She told herself she only wanted to help Thomas escape his predicament, but she couldn't deny that she enjoyed his attentions. And last night . . .

Her cheeks grew even warmer as her mind flickered through images of him looking at her with his eyes the color of a stormy sea. Holding her hands. Running a finger down her cheek.

"Caroline?" Penny stood in front of her. The group had disbanded and run off to prepare for the noon meal service. "Are you all right?"

"I . . ." Caroline grabbed Penny's hand, overcome with the desire to unburden herself. "May I speak with you for a moment? Alone?"

Penny glanced back at the other girls, preparing their stations.

"I promise it won't be but a minute."

Penny nodded, and Caroline led the way to the kitchen, and then outside. They were alone out here, but still Caroline took them several steps away from the kitchen door, just in case someone should come outside.

"Are you nervous?" Penny asked.

"Nervous? Oh! About being head waitress. Yes, some," she admitted. "But that's not what's on my mind."

Penny raised an eyebrow, a habit Caroline both envied and found slightly unladylike. A whistle pierced the air. The noon train had arrived.

Caroline twisted the edge of her apron in her hand, and then dropped it. The last thing she needed on her first day as head waitress was unsightly wrinkles. "Remember when I told you about Thomas?"

A devilish smile played across Penny's face. "How could I forget? Your tall, handsome, 'nice' man. I know that's where you went last night."

Caroline wished she could smile back, but her nerves were far too jumpy. She should've known Penny wouldn't have slept through her leaving their room so late. "You're right. But that wasn't what I wanted to confess to." She glanced off into the trees that hid the creek from sight. The leaves on the aspens and cottonwoods had turned even brighter and bolder, stark, warm colors against the gray sky. Maybe she should tell Penny about Thomas's problem before sharing how she felt about him. "There was something about Thomas I didn't tell you."

"Oh?" Penny's eyebrow crooked up again.

"He's . . ." She took a deep breath and fixed her gaze on Penny's kind green eyes. "He's wanted by the law."

Penny's smile fell. "He's an outlaw?"

"He isn't, really. Let me explain. At that restaurant on Sunday, remember the sheriff who came to our rescue? He's searching for Thomas."

“So Thomas is . . . What did that man call him?”

“Tom the Cat,” Caroline supplied. “But Penny—you have to believe me—he didn’t do what they think he did. At least, not part of it.”

“What is he wanted for?” Penny asked cautiously. “And for the love of all good things, please don’t tell me it’s murder.”

Caroline pushed her lips together. And nodded, just slightly.

Penny let out a frustrated sigh. “And you’ve been meeting with him in secret? He killed someone, Caroline! What are you thinking? Why didn’t you turn him in?”

“He was defending himself.” She told Penny a shortened version of Thomas’s unfortunate story.

“What does that matter for you? He’s a *wanted man*, Caroline. This isn’t going to end well for him.”

Caroline had never seen Penny look so reproachful. She wanted so badly to defend Thomas. Penny didn’t know how sweetly he’d made that picnic for her last night or about his dream to own a store. She didn’t know how hurt he was that someone would believe he was trying to steal. And she certainly didn’t know how remorseful he was that he’d killed someone. The grief he carried with him always sat just behind his easy smile and bright eyes. “You don’t know him,” she said softly.

“And you shouldn’t either,” Penny said. Her face softened when she saw Caroline’s jaw tremble. “Oh, no. You really care for him, don’t you?”

Caroline squeezed her eyes shut. And nodded. This was what she really wanted to share with Penny. “I shouldn’t. I know. But he’s so thoughtful, and he makes me feel . . . loved.”

“I’m sorry I encouraged you to break the rules,” Penny said. “I feel this is partly my fault.” She reached out for Caroline’s hands.

Caroline sniffed. “It’s not. This is all on me. Oh, Penny! I want to help him so badly. I want . . . I want . . .” What did she want? If she was truthful, she’d admit she wanted his arms around her again. She wanted him to say her name with such longing, it might split her heart in two. She wanted to see those eyes go dark when he looked at her. And she wanted, more than anything in the world, for him to be released from this shadow that followed him everywhere.

“You need to be strong right now.” Penny held her hands in between them. “We have a meal to serve, and you’re head waitress.”

"I know. But I'm not sure I can—"

"Nonsense. You *can*. Now dry your eyes. Concentrate on your work. And we'll talk more later about what to do with your Mr. Tom the Cat."

The name sent a shiver up Caroline's spine, as if by simply saying it, Penny was dooming Thomas to a life behind bars. "Please don't call him that."

Penny watched her for a moment, and then nodded. She let go of Caroline's hands, and Caroline reached into the pocket of her skirts for a handkerchief. Of course, the one that emerged was Thomas's. She dabbed at her eyes, returned the handkerchief, and straightened her skirts. "Do I look all right?"

"Put on a smile and no one will be any the wiser."

Caroline let a false smile lift her lips.

"Let's go, head waitress." Penny led the way back inside, and Caroline followed.

They emerged into the dining room with only a moment to spare. Dora found them, concern tracing her face. "I wasn't sure where you'd gone, so Millie and I prepared both of your stations."

"Thank you," Penny said, and Caroline echoed her.

What a way to begin her first service as head waitress, with her friend picking up her work. Caroline resolved to push Thomas from her mind and put all of her effort into her duties. She took her place next to Sarah and Mrs. Ruby in front of the other girls lined up in the dining room. It wasn't long before the first passengers streamed inside.

As soon as a couple was seated in her section, Caroline made her way toward them. Not three feet away, she stopped. Her heart flipped.

She knew these people.

Chapter Twenty-one

Thomas hadn't slept much the night before, and as afternoon stretched into evening, he began to feel it. He took his time putting away the tools and the leftover materials he'd used for repairs on the stables as the sun began to sink behind the mountains. Just as he set down the last piece of wood, the southbound train pulled out of Crest Stone station.

His stomach rumbled as he shut the door to the shed. He leaned against it and studied the hotel that lay several yards away. Caroline was in there, and most likely, he'd see her at supper. He'd skipped both breakfast and lunch inside, instead grabbing bread and cheese on his way out the door early this morning. It wasn't that he wanted to avoid her; it was that he was afraid he wouldn't be able to keep what had happened between them last night to himself. How could anyone look at him as he watched Caroline and not suspect his true feelings?

And then there was the nagging knowledge of what he'd realized last night—that he would need to go back to Barrett Mountain. He didn't know how but it had to happen soon, before Rayburn found him. Although how he was going to walk in there wanted for murder and then leave a free man was a mystery to Thomas. But it was the only way he'd ever be able to shake the charges against him. He had to take the chance. He dreaded telling Caroline. She wouldn't be happy with his decision, but he hoped she would at least understand. This was all too real, and too dangerous, and he didn't want her anywhere near it.

He stood outside for far longer than was necessary, until he was certain the Gilbert Girls indoors had cleaned up the dining room and eaten their own supper. Finally, when his stomach could stand it no longer, he entered the kitchen.

He stood there, blinking in the light of the lamps, and surveyed the room. Only the kitchen staff and a smattering of Gilbert Girls remained. He filled a plate of chicken, sweet potatoes, and bread and sat at the end of the table. The second he'd taken his first bite, someone sat down next to him. He glanced up, his mouth full, and nearly choked when he saw his table companion was none other than Caroline's friend—the tall one with the sharp eyes and the curls that refused to stay put behind her waitress's hat.

Thomas forced himself to keep chewing, which gave him plenty of time to wonder why in the world this woman had planted herself beside him and was now not-so-patiently waiting for him to acknowledge her. "Good evening," he said, finally, after swallowing the last of a hunk of bread.

"Good evening to you too, Mr. . . . I'm afraid I don't know your family name, sir." Her voice spoke of an upbringing somewhere down south, someplace more genteel than Thomas's own Texas.

"Drexel," he supplied.

She nodded. He waited for her to say something else, but she took her time, studying his face. He raised a glass of water to quench the dryness that suddenly parched his throat. Finally, she spoke. "I'm Miss May. I don't suppose you know that Miss Beauchamp and I are the closest of friends?"

Thomas nearly sputtered on his water. "Miss Beauchamp?"

"Don't play coy with me, Mr. Drexel," she said in a low voice. There were only a few others remaining at the table, all of them at the far end, but still, he appreciated her discretion. "Caroline and I tell each other everything."

"Oh?" He could think of nothing else to say. Did "everything" include how he hoped she'd felt about him after last night? *You fool*, he thought. His hopes had been colliding all day with the practical truth of what he needed to do. Of course, he hoped she'd wait for him, but he couldn't ask that of her. Especially when chances were high that he might not be able to return.

"Oh, yes." She eyed him like a stern older sister.

"I'm sorry, Miss May," he said, setting down his fork and returning her gaze. "I'm not sure what you want from me."

She glanced behind her at the handful of people at the table. "Perhaps we should remove our discussion to someplace more private?"

"I prefer not to lose my position here, thank you," he said. It came out colder than he'd intended, but he had the feeling Miss May didn't care for him one bit. And listening to a lecture from her about how he was ruining her friend's life was more than he could handle right now, with everything he was already facing.

She snorted. It was a most unladylike sound, but he presumed this woman didn't much care for what was ladylike and what was not. She was night and day from Caroline.

"I laugh, sir, because that seems to be the least of your concerns when it comes to Caroline."

She spoke the truth, and it hurt. "Please say what you need to here. It's unlikely we'll be overheard." He put a forkful of chicken into his mouth and chewed. It was flavorless and had the consistency of gruel. Although he imagined that had more to do with his current situation than the actual state of the food.

Miss May shrugged and leaned in closer. "Fine. My friend has feelings for you, as I'm sure you know."

He tried in vain to keep the smile from his face. He'd hoped Caroline felt the same way he did, but hearing her friend say it made him happier than he could have ever imagined.

"But I know, as does she, of course, that you aren't exactly in a position to court any woman."

His fork stilled over his food as what he'd already eaten went rock solid in his stomach. "What do you mean?"

"I'm certain you know what I'm saying, Tom the Cat." Miss May's voice was barely a whisper, and yet it seemed she'd screamed those last three words.

Thomas pushed his plate away. "Did she tell you about the entire sordid affair?"

"Enough to understand that she believes you are innocent."

He swallowed. "Do—"

Miss May didn't let him speak. "Listen, Mr. Drexel. I don't particularly care if you're innocent or guilty. All I care about is Caroline. And if you or anything about your situation hurts her in any way, I can't promise I'll continue to keep your little secret." She tilted her head and looked him straight in the eyes. This woman was no wilting flower, that much was for certain. "And don't think I'm afraid of you."

Thomas sighed and rubbed his hands over his face. "You have no need to fear me. I'm not the man those posters make me out to be."

"I don't care one whit. I only want your reassurance that none of this will touch Caroline."

Her words hit that exact spot in the back of his mind—the place where he'd shoved the fear that he might not return to her. "You have my word." His voice sounded hollow, as if he'd carved out the inside of it and tossed it away, along with any chance at happiness. Why should he give Caroline hope that he would come back when the odds were against him? And yet . . . he couldn't imagine not clinging to that one little bit of light in his life.

"Good." She eyed him for a moment before standing. "Thank you for hearing me out."

He nodded a welcome, and she disappeared from the kitchen. No longer hungry, he dropped the rest of his food into the scrap bin before handing the plate, utensils, and glass to the boy washing dishes. And then he stepped out into the dark evening, hoping to draw a full breath again.

It didn't work. All his thoughts about what Miss May had said, what he knew he should do, the death sentence hanging over him if he wasn't successful, and the unquestionable desire to simply run *now* with Caroline's hand in his own—none of these worries would let him steady his breathing or even think a full thought.

It was a lovely night—cold but clear, the moon shining overhead, and quiet. Just like that night he'd ridden away from the mining town. Perhaps a ride was what he needed to clear his head. Thomas made his way across brown grasses to the new stables he'd been repairing earlier. They sat where the building crew's tents used to reside.

The moment he stepped inside, a voice spoke softly.

Caroline.

Chapter Twenty-two

"You look like you wouldn't hurt a fly, would you?" Caroline cooed to the small dappled gray horse housed at the end of the stables. The horse nickered and nuzzled her arm. She'd come in here to sort through the tumbling thoughts she couldn't focus on while serving the evening meal. Horses were soothing—when she wasn't on one of them. Although, she reflected, she'd done well when riding with Thomas last night. Perhaps she should attempt to ride alone again. This gray horse with eyelashes as long as the wisps of hair that framed Caroline's face didn't seem the sort of horse who would toss her.

The hinges on the stable door squealed. Caroline yanked her head up just in time to see the moonlit outline of the door disappear as it was shut. Someone was in here with her.

Heart knocking against her ribs, Caroline shrunk into the corner of the horse's stall. It was past dinner, and dark out. Who would be in the stables this late? She cast her eyes around furtively for a weapon. The only thing she could reach was a horse brush. And what good would that do her? She supposed she could throw it at the person, if she needed to. She carefully stretched out her arm and snatched it from the side of the stall.

"Caroline?" a male voice called. Thomas.

Caroline exhaled, her body shuddering as the fear left her. Although after what had happened at the noon meal, she wasn't sure she was ready to see Thomas, as much as her heart said otherwise. But there was no use hiding back here. She emerged from the stall, closing the door behind her.

"What are you doing here?" he asked, leaning against a post that sat between two stalls.

"I . . ." She cast about for the best way to answer. She was no liar, after all, despite the falsehoods she'd already told today. "I needed to think. And this seemed a likely place to do so."

He nodded as if he understood. "What is it that's weighing on your mind?"

Caroline reached over the door of the stall next to them and scratched the nose of a chestnut mare. The simple action helped her gather her courage. "Two of my family's acquaintances were at lunch today." She closed her eyes for a moment as it rushed back to her.

She had approached the well-dressed couple to welcome them to the Crest Stone and take their order. When they looked up at her, she knew she was in trouble.

The woman, dripping in jewelry, narrowed her eyes in recognition before allowing a confused smile to cross her face. "Miss Beauchamp? Caroline! My dear, whatever are you doing here? And in such . . ." She waved her hand at Caroline's gray-and-white Gilbert Company dress.

Her husband, who had clearly not recognized Caroline at all, had simply sat there, a polite smile on his face.

Caroline couldn't think of what to say. How could she explain this? And more importantly, how could she keep this woman, Mrs. Flynn, from sending a telegram to her parents immediately?

Before she could speak, Mrs. Flynn said, "Your mother told me you were visiting relatives in the New York countryside."

"Yes . . ." Caroline finally managed to say. Her heart beat triple-time. She needed some way to convince this woman that she was supposed to be here, and yet not alarm her enough to send her to the hotel's telegraph office. She needed a lie. "My . . . aunt. She wanted to see the country. And so we are traveling." The words tasted like sawdust in her mouth.

"Where is she? I'd so like to meet her." Mrs. Flynn glanced around the dining room.

"Oh, she's not here. She is . . . indisposed. Not feeling quite herself." Caroline forced herself to keep her hands at her sides and her eyes locked with Mrs. Flynn's. The lies felt like rocks, filling her skirts and pulling her down to drown.

"Too bad, too bad," Mr. Flynn said, although he mostly looked as if he'd prefer to get his hands on the soup at the nearby tables.

"I understand. These long rail journeys can test the heartiest of us. But darling—" Mrs. Flynn took Caroline's hand and lifted her arm. "Why are you dressed like one of the serving girls?"

This would be the hardest one of all. The lie coiled up, snakelike, and wove its way into words. "I spilled soup on my skirts. An entire bowl! We'd already sent all of our clothing to be laundered. One of these ladies was kind enough to lend me a dress."

Mrs. Flynn said nothing, but her eyes drifted to the cap on Caroline's head. Nothing in her fabricated story could explain why she was wearing it.

Caroline reached for the hat, about to pull it from her hair. But that would be against the rules. Gilbert Girls were expected to be fully uniformed while working, and here she was, the head waitress, ready to break that rule right in the middle of the dining room. Her hand fluttered down as she searched for an explanation.

Mrs. Flynn studied her again and gave her the pretense of a smile. "This is the most odd situation," she said, almost to herself.

"I must get back to my table."

"Yes, you must."

"Good evening, miss." Mr. Flynn stood and bowed.

Caroline nodded in return. "Good evening to you, too." And then she walked as quickly as possible to her station, where she gripped the doorframe for support and breathed as if she'd just run here straight from Boston. She couldn't continue to wait the tables in her section, not with the Flynns right there. When Dora came to check on her, Caroline persuaded her to switch sections. Dora's occupied the far end of the room, near the entryway. Hopefully from there, Caroline would blend into the other girls with their matching dresses. All she had to do was mention the word Boston to Dora, and her friend understood.

And now she found herself explaining what had happened to Thomas. "They're certainly going to telegraph my family. They probably already have."

"Perhaps. What would happen then?" he asked.

A weight sat on Caroline's chest, even thinking about that. "I don't know. They may send someone for me. My father, or maybe my brother." She didn't say who else that someone could be. She prayed it wasn't the man she'd escaped by coming here. If it was, they were both in danger. The last thing she ever wanted was her past hurting Thomas, but that was a distinct possibility now. She could barely breathe, thinking about it.

"If that happens, you tell him you don't wish to return home and you won't enter an engagement with the man they chose." Thomas made it sound so easy. When it wasn't, at all. He must have noticed the troubled look on her face, because he reached for her hand.

She let him take it, and oh, how she wanted him to draw her close and hold her.

But she couldn't. It was wrong of her to allow anything like that before, and now, having seen the Flynns, the reality of the situation she'd left behind in Boston became even more stark.

Her heart was not her own to give away.

And to pretend to Thomas that it was, that was not only a lie itself, it was cruel. It didn't matter how she felt toward him at all. And it was cruel to put him in harm's way.

Caroline pulled her hand from his grip. He didn't resist but his face registered surprise.

"Did I hurt you?" he asked.

Her heart cracked in two. "No, of course not. It's . . ." The shame of what she'd done to him rushed through her entire body. "I can't. I'm sorry," she whispered.

She darted around him and out the door of the stables.

"Caroline?" she heard him call. His voice on her name pierced her soul. With tears streaming down her cheeks, she ignored it.

She didn't stop running until she was inside her room.

Chapter Twenty-three

Thomas tugged at his necktie. The thing felt as if it were choking him. But if he wanted to eat in the dining room, he needed to dress the part. He hovered near the entrance to the dining room, waiting to see which section was Caroline's. After just a few seconds, he spotted her midway through the room. One table remained open in her section, and he walked as fast as he could without drawing attention to himself.

He'd never eaten in here before. His wallet would certainly feel it by the end of the meal, but it was worth it to talk to Caroline. He'd seen her here and there throughout the week since she'd turned and run from him, and not once had she even acknowledged him, much less spoken to him. The calloused part of his heart told him she'd been fooling him all along, and as soon as she realized he had real feelings for her, she knew her game was up. She thought she was too good for him, just like his mother had felt about his father.

But as easy as those thoughts were to fall into, something else nagged at him. The sheer honesty in her face when she looked at him. Her tears by the creek. The earnest way she'd said she wanted to help him. How she'd sighed when he touched her face.

It didn't make any sense, and since Caroline refused to even look at him, he'd decided to put himself in a position where she had to speak to him. He not only needed to find out what was wrong, but he also needed to tell her of his plans to return to Barrett Mountain. He decided he would ask her to wait. It felt selfish, but besides his freedom, she was the only thing he wanted.

And if she said no . . . well, he wouldn't be surprised. Not with the way she'd acted toward him all week. Still, he hoped. If he laid out his heart for her, then maybe the Caroline he knew would agree to be there for him.

He pretended to study the menu, written in flourishing script on a heavy piece of cream-colored paper, until she arrived.

"Good afternoon, sir. I trust your journey has been—" Caroline stopped talking the second he looked up. She glanced furiously to either side of her, as if to ensure no one else was looking at them. "What are you doing here?"

"Having a meal, like all of these other fine folk. Now, do you recommend the rabbit or the beef stew? I can't seem to make up my mind." He gave her what he hoped was a teasing smile, just like the ones that used to make her straighten up and get all sniffy with him when he first met her, and that later made her smile.

She did neither. Instead she clasped her hands around her water pitcher and met his gaze. Her eyes looked duller than normal, sad even, rather than their usual cheerful blue. "I've asked Mrs. Ruby for a transfer."

Thomas stilled. "What do you mean?"

She drew a deep breath. "I asked her to let the company know I would like to transfer to another hotel. The telegram came today. I'll report to a Gilbert hotel in California at the end of next week."

"Why?" was the only word Thomas could seem to get out of his mouth. The air all seemed to have left the room.

She pressed her lips together. "I recommend the beef stew. It has a lovely flavor."

"I don't care about the menu." He spoke so harshly that Caroline flinched. "I'm sorry." He desperately wanted to take her hand, but that was impossible here in front of everyone. "You haven't spoken to me all week. And now this? Please, tell me why you're leaving. I deserve to know that much."

"Miss? Miss, may I have some more water?" A man at the next table held up his glass.

Caroline closed her eyes for a half-second. "I'll return. I can't leave my customers waiting."

Thomas sat impatiently while Caroline refilled water and lemonade and tea, took orders, and brought food to her tables. She set a steaming bowl of beef stew in front of him. It might have been a bowl of sawdust, for all the appetite Thomas had. She paused by his table a moment before speaking.

"I need to leave Crest Stone before someone comes for me." She brushed nonexistent crumbs from his tablecloth. "I've informed Mrs. Ruby that I wish my family not to find me."

Her face looked as if it hadn't smiled since before those people she knew from Boston had arrived here. Thomas wished he could take all of that away from her. He wished he could make her smile all the time. But none of what she said explained why she'd been so cold toward him.

"I see," he said, although he didn't at all. "Why didn't you confide in me?"

She closed her eyes for a split second, dragging in a breath before opening them again. "This is my business to handle, Mr. Drexel."

It was as if she'd taken his heart and thrown it into his face. A thousand different feelings raged inside him, but instead of acknowledging any of them, he said, "I'm going back to Barrett Mountain. I wanted you to know."

Her eyes widened. "That's far too dangerous."

"I have no other choice. I'll stay low. All I need to do is search the area and then speak to a few folks."

She still looked petrified—for him. A tiny sliver of hope worked its way back into Thomas's heart.

"I have to do this," he said. "It's the only chance I have at clearing my name. I'll leave tomorrow, first thing in the morning. I would have gone sooner, but I wanted to see you first." He hoped those words implied everything he meant.

Caroline took a tiny step backward. She was doing exactly as he'd done these past several months. Hiding. Running. Refusing to face a problem.

"I don't think you should leave," he said. "I . . ." He cleared his throat. "I wanted to ask you if you'd wait for me. Here."

"I have no choice." Her voice was barely a whisper.

"You do." Thomas's voice rose. He forced himself to lower it. "You encouraged me to do what I needed to prove my innocence. Well, now it's your turn."

"My turn to do what exactly?" She glanced at her other tables, ever the head waitress. The woman he knew was in there, inside this scared, cold person who stood beside him now.

"You're running away to hide again. If you ever want to be free of your family, you need to face them and tell them that."

"It's not that simple," she said, her face even paler than usual.

"Of course it isn't. Just as choosing to return to the last place I should be isn't simple either. But if I can do that, you can tell your family what you really want."

"You don't understand." She cast her eyes to the richly carpeted floor.

"No, I don't." It came out frustrated. "You're more courageous than you know, Caroline. You need to step forward and embrace that."

He could see her swallow, and he hoped—he almost prayed—she'd agree.

"I must attend to my other tables." She smoothed her pristine apron. "Thomas—Mr. Drexel—I ask you please not to follow me to California. I . . . I do not wish to see you again."

With a swish of her skirts, she was gone, leaving Thomas stunned with a cooling bowl of stew and a heart that felt covered in frost.

He'd been wrong about her. He threw his napkin on the table, fished a few bills from his pocket to join the napkin, and left. He refused to chase after a woman who didn't truly love him. If she did, she'd send word to her family admitting where she was and telling them she refused to marry the man they'd chosen. And then if her father came here, Thomas would stand by her side and set him straight. Instead, she was going to run, to leave Thomas behind. She wasn't at all who he'd thought she was. And if that was the case, then good riddance.

Perhaps Caroline had just done him the biggest favor of his life.

Chapter Twenty-four

"You're *leaving*?" Penny's incredulous voice announced Caroline's decision to the entire dormitory.

"But why?" Millie asked, from where she and Dora stood near the door to their friends' room.

Caroline sighed. "It's not immediate. Mrs. Ruby said it could take up to two weeks."

"You didn't answer Millie's question," Dora said in her soft voice.

"I . . . I need a change." Caroline forced a smile at her friends. But it was too much. She sunk down onto her bed with her face in her hands. All she could think of was Thomas's face when she'd told him not to follow her. She couldn't have hurt him more if she'd shot him. And now her friends . . . In her rush to ask Mrs. Ruby for a transfer before her family could find her, Caroline hadn't even thought of them. What kind of friend was she?

Penny spoke in hushed tones to the other two girls, and then the door shut. Caroline felt her sit on the bed. Neither of them said a word for a few minutes until Caroline finally looked up.

"I had to do it," she said, her eyes wet with unshed tears.

Penny tilted her head. "Because of Mr. Drexel? Did he hurt you? I warned him—"

"No! No, he did nothing." Nothing except be there for her every single time she needed him. "Wait, you spoke with him?"

Guilt flitted across Penny's face. "I'm sorry. I wanted to ensure he wasn't a rake. I told him he'd regret it if he hurt you in any way."

Caroline smiled and swiped a tear from her face. "You're the best friend I ever could have asked for."

"Then why in the world are you leaving?" Penny leaned forward, bracing herself with a hand against the bed. "We were having such fun together here, with Dora and all the other girls. Think of the adventures we'll never have now!"

Caroline twisted her apron. "It's my family," she said quietly.

"Did they ask you to return? How did they find you?"

The cotton bunched and wrinkled under Caroline's hands. She'd told her friends only the very simplest details of why she'd left home.

"Caroline?" Penny laid a hand on her arm.

"There was a couple in the dining room about a week ago. Friends of my family. They recognized me. I'm certain they wired my father before they left. It won't be long until . . . someone comes looking for me."

"So let them!" Penny declared. "You'll just tell your father that you prefer to remain here, and you refuse to marry that old man back in Boston. I'll stand with you, if you need me. I'm sure any of the other girls will too. And Mrs. Ruby! She can't be happy she's losing her head waitress so soon."

Caroline shook her head. "I can't."

"You can too. You're braver than you think."

Those words—nearly an echo of what Thomas said to her just a couple of hours ago—nearly knocked the breath from Caroline. In truth, if that was all there was to it, she might be able to do such a thing.

"You don't understand," she said. "I can't be found."

Penny's eyes crinkled as she took in the look on Caroline's face. "Would your father hurt you?"

"No." *Not my father*, she thought. It wouldn't be just her feeling that wrath, but Thomas too. And that, she could never live with. "But I need to leave. Soon."

"I wish you'd tell me more," Penny said.

The heaviness of it all engulfed Caroline like a bucket of water overturned on her head. She'd done the right thing last spring, that was one thing of which she was certain. She'd had no other choice—no real one. But it was her burden to bear, and she wouldn't force the consequences of her decision onto anyone else. It weighed her down, and the last thing she felt like doing was talking about it anymore.

"I'm tired." Caroline jumped up and began undressing for bed.

Penny sat for a moment on the bed, as if she were waiting for more. When it was clear Caroline wasn't offering any further explanation, Penny gave a great sigh and stood. They prepared for bed in silence.

But after they'd doused the lamp and Penny's breathing softened into a regular rhythm, Caroline lay still, wide awake. Every time she closed her eyes, Thomas's hurt face appeared. She'd done what she needed to, she reminded herself. It would hurt him far less to lose her now than it would to find out she was far more indebted to that monster of a man in Boston than she'd told him. And that his life would be in danger if that same man found out about her feelings for Thomas.

But as unable as she was to promise him her heart, she'd meant every word she'd said to him before today.

It was for the best, she tried to tell herself. He'd asked her to wait for him. Her heart had nearly shattered on the spot. She wanted so badly to say yes. But what if he was unable to clear his name? What if he returned to Barrett Mountain and was arrested on the spot? It was better for her to remain alone, where she would always have her work with the Gilbert Company.

She repeated those thoughts to herself over and over, but still, the doubt crept in.

Was she doing the right thing?

As sleep started to filter in around the edges of her consciousness, a sharp rap on the door made her sit upright in bed.

"Who is that?" Penny asked, her voice tinged with sleep.

"Girls?" Mrs. Ruby's voice called from outside their door. "I'm sorry to wake you, but there is an urgent visitor here for Caroline."

Caroline's heart hammered. An urgent visitor could mean only one person.

The last man she ever wanted to lay eyes on again.

Chapter Twenty-five

The mining encampment a few miles east of Crest Stone seemed a good enough place to lose himself, but Thomas couldn't even mange to do that correctly. He folded the hand he was dealt and left the table, out of money and still wondering exactly how he'd manage to fall for someone like Caroline.

At least he'd gathered the courage to search for a way to clear his name. He had that much to thank her for. He leaned against the bar—which wasn't but a plank over stacks of stones. The saloon itself was a rickety building, one of the few among a town of canvasses and tents. Between the hastily constructed wooden plats that made up the walls, a man could see lamps flickering along the dirt road outside.

The bartender poured Thomas a whiskey he suspected was heavily watered down. He didn't drink much, and although now seemed the perfect time to pick up such a habit, he couldn't gather the taste for it. Instead, he cupped the glass and stared into the amber liquid as if it might have all the answers to his problems. First, how he was going to get into the Barrett Mountain camp without being recognized. Second, whether all this effort would be worthwhile. And third, whether he'd ever be able to erase the mark Caroline left on his soul.

A woman laughed from across the room, drawing Thomas's eyes up from his full glass. Her hair was the same shade of ripened wheat as Caroline's, but the similarities ended there. This woman was dolled up in rouge, ringlets, and ruffled skirts that Thomas suspected would look less grand in daylight than they did in the flickering lamplight and shadows of the saloon.

Caroline had worn real finery at one point in her life. She'd also probably done her hair in ringlets and played the coquette. He tried to picture her like that, acting as his mother might have. It made the hurt ease a little. At least until the memory of her happy face at their cabin picnic, or the light in her eyes when she suggested he might be able to find proof of his innocence, surfaced. Then, the pain flooded in anew.

It made no sense. How could that woman be the same as the one who'd snubbed him today? The one who may as well have been dressed in her Boston frippery, trilling out laughter to the richest man at the party and unable to speak her mind to her own family. These two versions of her didn't match, and he couldn't wrap his mind around it.

Does it matter? Would she have waited for you anyway? He was better off alone. Once he got the law off his back, he'd be free to save money and open his own store somewhere. It could be anywhere he wanted. He'd find some new town, just starting out, and establish himself as a proprietor. *A pillar of the community*, Caroline had said.

Thomas let out an angry sigh. It seemed she snuck into every thought he had. The things she'd said, the way she'd looked at him through her lashes, the blush on her cheeks when he'd teased her, the soft warmth of her skin. He wouldn't have even remembered he wanted to run a store until she'd asked him.

He pushed the full glass back onto the bar with a little more force than was necessary. The whiskey sloshed out a bit, but Thomas was already headed to the door. He'd been wasting time sitting here and bemoaning his situation. Instead, he'd return to the hotel, pack, and inform McFarland of his plans first thing in the morning.

And then he'd be off to pursue his innocence before Rayburn could find him. If he was lucky, he might even be able to outrun his memories of Caroline.

Chapter Twenty-six

Caroline's hands shook as she dressed. Penny had asked approximately two hundred questions, all of which Caroline refused to answer, and so now, Penny sat stubbornly on her bed, refusing to sleep until Caroline returned from this midnight meeting.

Her fingers fumbled on the buttons of her nicest dress, a soft pink silk edged in small pleats. She feared what Mrs. Ruby thought she knew. There was no possibility of the strict woman allowing a visit from an unrelated male to the women's dormitory at any time, and particularly not at this unconscionable hour. If her visitor told Mrs. Ruby they were married, however . . . Caroline put a hand to her chest as bile seared her throat. She closed her eyes for a moment and wished she'd already received her transfer.

You're more courageous than you know. Thomas's words—and later, Penny's—echoed through her head. She knew she had courage inside her somewhere. Not many women of her station would have the gall to leave home without a word, board a train alone, and traverse the country, only to emerge in the most godforsaken place where she was then expected to work as she'd never done in her life.

But yet, she'd done just that.

And although pride was a sin, Caroline was *proud* of what she'd accomplished. She stretched her fingers out until they stopped shaking, then stood up as tall as she could and glanced into the small glass on the dressing table.

"Caroline?" Penny said as Caroline reached for the doorknob. "I'm here if you need me."

Caroline wanted nothing more than to run back and wrap her arms around her friend. But if she did that, she'd lose every ounce of courage she'd gathered to face what she must. "Thank you. You don't know how much that means to me." And with that, she left to face her fate.

Mrs. Ruby was waiting for her in the hallway. "He said it was urgent, or else I would have made him wait until a more proper time."

"It's quite all right," Caroline murmured. She felt as if she were marching to her own funeral as she walked with Mrs. Ruby toward the parlor the girls used near the second-floor landing. The door was open, and Mrs. Ruby paused to let Caroline go inside.

She drew a deep breath, even as she was struck by the fiercest longing to turn on her heels and run right back to her room.

Inside, a tall man with neatly combed strawberry blond hair, a once-impeccable suit that was now creased and dotted with specks of dirt, and an air of impatience rose from one of the chairs when she entered.

"Quentin?" Caroline grasped the doorframe to steady herself. "I— I didn't expect you."

Her older brother raised his perfectly groomed eyebrows. "No, I suppose you didn't. How have you been, sister?"

"I am well, thank you. And you?" The formality of the moment was about to strangle Caroline. Perhaps she really was of the West now.

"I've been better. I've had very little sleep since leaving Boston, and the driver and wagon I hired for this last leg of the journey were less than desirable."

"Why didn't you take the train?" It wasn't what she wanted to ask him, but it allowed her time to compose herself. Of course, she wasn't happy her brother had found her, but it was better than the man she had been expecting.

"Blasted thing only runs twice a day." Upon seeing the surprised look on her face, he added, "I apologize. The lack of gentility around here must be affecting me."

"The Crest Stone Hotel is quite civilized," she informed him.

"I'm certain it is," he said, although the tone of his voice said otherwise. He paced the room, stopping to examine a clock on the mantel of the fireplace, which still held embers from earlier in the evening. "We were all happy to receive the telegram from Mr. and Mrs. Flynn. Mother cried upon learning you were safe."

Guilt shot through Caroline in a way it hadn't since she'd left. "Mother cried?"

Quentin gave a short laugh. "Hard to believe, I know." He crossed the room and took up her hand. "We were all overjoyed to learn where you were."

Caroline stared at his gloved hands covering hers. "I am sorry for any worry I caused you or the family. But I'm not at all sorry I left."

Her brother breathed out heavily. "It was quite a dramatic response to your engagement."

Even the mere word made Caroline feel as if she were slowly sinking. She forced herself to breathe. This could be much worse, after all. Her brother could be reasoned with. She looked up at him. "I never asked to be married."

"I don't understand. Don't you wish to have your own family? Your own household?"

"Not with that man." Her words were raw, and she wished, more than anything, for Quentin to understand.

"Mr. Wiltshire?" He tilted his head as if he'd heard her incorrectly. "Father pulled many a string to make that match happen. You couldn't ask for a more prominent family or a more established business to be marrying into. You'd want for nothing."

"Quentin." Caroline placed her free hand on top of her brother's. "Surely you've heard the rumors."

"Ridiculous. The man has been unlucky."

She shook her head. "I fear there's truth to them. I *know* there is truth to them." How else could she explain the bruises lurking beneath the layers of powder on the late Mrs. Wiltshire's face at last year's Christmas parties? Or the way, a couple of years before that, the first Mrs. Wiltshire developed a limp not long after she'd been married? Quentin didn't notice those things, but the ladies did. They took note, and when each of Mr. Wiltshire's wives passed away in tragic, unexpected ways, they prayed none of them were next in line.

Caroline's prayers hadn't been answered, at least not in the way she'd hoped. So instead, she'd taken it upon herself to avoid becoming the third Mrs. Wiltshire.

"You are being unreasonable. Father sent me here to fetch you home, where you'll fulfill the contract you signed and be married."

Caroline pulled her hands from his. "I will do no such thing." Then, seeing the astounded look on her brother's face, she composed herself back into the diminutive creature he expected her to be. She'd need to prevail on his sentiments. "Please, Quentin. If I marry that man, I won't live another year."

"That's preposterous. What are you going to do instead? Live out here in the wilderness? Work as a waitress for the rest of your life? Die a spinster? You signed a contract, after all. You can't marry some ruffian cowboy."

Thomas's hurt face appeared in her mind again. What did she have left here? Certainly not him. She'd seen to that. She had her work here, or in California, if she chose. And despite the distaste with which Quentin said the word *waitress*, Caroline was proud of her work.

Quentin laid a hand on her arm. More softly, he said, "You know Father won't rest until you're returned and married. Not only for his reputation, but for the good of the company."

The company. That was it. The reason he'd sell his own daughter into marriage with a snake such as Mr. Wiltshire. Quentin was right. She'd never have a moment's peace, not as long as Father was alive. And certainly not as long as Mr. Wiltshire wanted her. She'd spend her life hiding.

Like Thomas.

She closed her eyes as the loss of it all threatened to consume her again. It was for Thomas's own good. She was engaged, part of a contract in which her marriage would infuse funding into her family's company, and therefore, she couldn't in good conscience give her heart to another man. And she'd feared what would happen to Thomas if Mr. Wiltshire at all suspected she had feelings for him. She'd already let him go. He could find a woman who was free to be with him once he'd proven his innocence. She couldn't contemplate what would happen to him if he didn't succeed. And she . . .

What would she do? Run forever?

"At least come stay with me in Cañon City. You can think more on it there." Quentin scooped up his top hat from the end table, as if the matter was already decided.

And perhaps it was. A cold sense of resignation settled around Caroline's heart. "Let me pack my things."

Chapter Twenty-seven

The sun had barely begun tracing the sky when Thomas awoke the next morning. He'd hardly slept, having dreamt of faceless men chasing him and of Caroline. As he dressed he realized he needed to do two things: tell McFarland why he was leaving and see Caroline one last time.

The first, he should have done long ago, as Caroline had told him. If McFarland understood, Thomas would be on his way. And if he didn't, then he'd simply need to make a quicker escape. But in his heart, he knew McFarland only hired men he trusted. He'd seen something in Thomas, and it was only right that Thomas repay that trust with the truth.

After that, he'd see Caroline and tell her that he'd come clean to McFarland. He'd ask again if she'd wait until he returned. If she still decided she'd rather transfer, then so be it. But if she waited . . . he dared not hope. All last night in that saloon, he'd tried to reconcile the woman he thought he'd known with the woman she'd shown him yesterday. He couldn't do it. One of them was the true Caroline, and he wouldn't let her go until he knew which she was. And if she wasn't the woman he'd thought she was, he'd leave her be.

Thomas surveyed his meager belongings. It wouldn't take long to pack them up. He planned to be on the evening train from Santa Fe to Cañon City. From Cañon City, he'd continue north to Colorado City. There, he'd hire a horse and ride into the mountains.

He knocked on McFarland's door at exactly eight o'clock. The man himself answered, knotting his tie. "Drexel! What can I do for you this fine morning?" he asked in his light brogue.

Thomas glanced around the room. Mrs. McFarland was nowhere to be seen, which was fine by him. He'd rather she not hear of his alleged misdeeds. "I need to speak with you a moment."

McFarland gestured at the two wing chairs that sat opposite each other in front of the glowing fireplace. Thomas welcomed the heat as he sat.

"What's on your mind, son?"

Thomas warmed at the affectionate term, although he wondered if McFarland would feel the same way about him once he shared his secret. "I need to leave for a brief time, but would like to return if you'll have me."

"Leave?" McFarland's brow crinkled.

Thomas forced himself to keep eye contact with his boss. "I need to return to the mining town where I worked prior to coming to Crest Stone. I have . . . unfinished business there I need to resolve."

McFarland nodded, but said nothing.

Thomas could tell he was waiting for more. "This isn't easy to own up to, but I ran into a bit of trouble up there before I left." He was beginning to sweat, but he refused to shift positions. Instead, he pushed forward and told McFarland the whole terrible story, including running away instead of facing the law. "I understand if you'd prefer to turn me in right now," he finished. Thomas steeled himself, hoping this wasn't the option McFarland chose.

The older man tapped a hand against his leg. "I'll do no such thing. I can tell you're a decent sort of man, Drexel. I believe you should have stayed and cleared your name when this happened, but I also understand the facts were against you. If you weren't already planning to return and handle the situation now, I'd encourage you to do just that."

Thomas relaxed. It was just as Caroline had said. He should have come forward sooner, but perhaps it was better he'd waited. After all, now he was determined to return and end this nonsense of running away. A few weeks ago, he couldn't have said the same, and he imagined McFarland may not have been so charitable toward his frame of mind then.

"I'll hold your position for you until the end of the year," McFarland said, standing.

Thomas followed suit. "Thank you, sir."

"And please, don't hesitate to send word if you need anything from me." He clapped Thomas on the back. "Good luck, son. I hope to see you back here soon."

Thomas left McFarland's apartment feeling lighter than he had in a long time. Perhaps there was truth in that old saying—*the truth will set you free*. He only hoped his meeting with Caroline would go just as well.

The morning passed slowly, and Thomas occupied himself with finishing up work on the stables. Finally, the noon train from Cañon City arrived, and Thomas joined the passengers and some of the hotel guests in the dining room for a meal. Paying for his food was the only way he knew he'd be able to see Caroline. He stood near the door, looking for her. A minute passed, then two, then three. Gilbert Girls hustled to and from the kitchen and their serving stations, but there was no sign of his small, light-haired beauty.

He spotted Miss May, and preparing himself for another telling-off, approached her as she carried a steaming pot of tea to her station. "Miss May, I hate to interrupt your work, but could you tell me where Miss Beauchamp is this afternoon?"

She cupped the pot with a small towel in her free hand and frowned. "She's left."

The words took him aback. She'd said it would take at least two weeks for her transfer to come through. "What do you mean?"

Miss May regarded him with something between suspicion and pity, as if she couldn't make up her mind whether she liked or distrusted him. "Her brother arrived late last night. They left immediately for Cañon City." She set the pot down before turning to look back at Thomas. "She told me she might be traveling to Boston, but she wouldn't say more."

"Boston?" The word nearly knocked Thomas over. "That makes no sense. She went to so much effort to leave home."

"I know." Miss May cast her eyes about the dining room before returning them to Thomas. "Did you say something to her?"

He shook his head. He couldn't imagine her returning voluntarily to Boston, not after what she'd told him.

"Honestly, Mr. Drexel, I'm worried about her."

"I'll send word," he said so fast the words ran into each other. When Miss May cocked her head in confusion, he added, "I'm leaving myself, but I'll stop in Cañon City first and find Caroline."

Miss May's expression relaxed. "Thank you."

He inclined his head, then made his way out of the dining room without eating. He needed to return to his room, gather his things, and figure out what he was going to say to Caroline when he saw her. Even if she wanted nothing to do with him, she couldn't go to Boston. Not after the effort she'd made to leave and start a life here. He couldn't let her give all of that up.

Thomas strode across the lobby through the people milling there, waiting to board the train or for a seat to empty at the nearby lunch counter. Turning past the front desk, he almost collided with a gentleman who was waiting to speak with the clerk.

"Well, if it ain't who I've been looking for."

Thomas's heart went cold as he realized exactly who it was he'd run into. Deputy Frank Rayburn. Now Sheriff Frank Rayburn.

Run. The word surfaced in Thomas's mind as Rayburn held up a set of irons.

He eyeballed a path from his current position to the door. He could run. Or he could face his fate.

Thomas took a step back.

Chapter Twenty-eight

The hotel room was likely the finest in Cañon City, but still it was not the sort of place to which Caroline's brother was accustomed. He'd been appalled that the front desk clerk would simply allow visitors to knock on their door, instead of sending someone up to announce that a visitor had arrived. After that had happened once, he'd nearly berated the poor clerk into a sniveling mess. No one had arrived unannounced since then.

And visitors they'd had aplenty in the two days they'd been there. Caroline had pled indecisiveness, telling Quentin she needed to be certain she wanted to return home. Truthfully, she'd made up her mind but sought to put off the consequences of her decision for a bit longer. Quentin had agreed to stay until the end of the week. He'd wired their father—and most likely the dreadful Mr. Wiltshire—that he had been successful in finding Caroline. And now he was taking the opportunity to make business contacts in Cañon City.

"In a few years' time, these dusty towns will be bustling cities, and the country will be crisscrossed with railway tracks," he'd said to Caroline. "And Beauchamp Imports will be the ideal company to get goods to these people. Can you imagine how we'd grow?"

Caroline had nodded politely. It made sense, and so she tolerated the steady stream of mercantile owners, government officials, and railway men who'd visited their rooms. It was a nice distraction from the heavy thoughts weighing on her.

Her impending marriage. The life she'd created for herself here. Her friends. Thomas. It all flooded into her mind whenever she had a moment alone. The rest of the time, she shoved any emotions that rose right back down. She was becoming adept at stoicism.

So when a knock sounded on their door again late in the afternoon, Caroline thankfully put aside the book she was attempting—and failing—to read and rose to greet the clerk.

"I'm so sorry, miss. This woman, she wouldn't stay downstairs, and I know your brother is—I'm so sorry." The flustered clerk threw up his hands as Penny barged right past him and into Caroline's room.

"It's quite all right," Caroline said, as soon as the shock of seeing her friend appear here wore off. "I'm not as hard to please as my brother." She gave him a benevolent smile, and he relaxed just a little.

"The thing is," he said, tapping nervous fingers against his trousers, "there are more of them downstairs."

"Oh, for the love of all that's good," Penny said from behind Caroline. "There are only two. Please send them up."

Caroline glanced at Penny, her eyebrows raised in a question.

"Dora and Millie."

Caroline turned back to the clerk and nodded, then shut the door.

"Are you all right? Have you been hurt?" Penny fussed as she took both of Caroline's hands in her own and held them out to the sides.

"No, of course not." Caroline shook off her grip. "Why are you here?"

Penny let out a frustrated sound. "To ensure you haven't completely lost your mind. Now, where's that no-good brother of yours? I have words for him."

"He isn't here," Caroline said, thankful Quentin had gone out to meet yet another shop owner. He was due back in about an hour. They were to have dinner in the restaurant downstairs with the town mayor, the local sheriff, and a few businessmen.

Penny had already crossed the room, peeking into the nearby bedrooms. "Hmph. Did Mr. Drexel come to see you?"

Caroline slowly shook her head. She'd hurt Thomas to ensure he'd leave her alone. And it appeared that plan had worked, as much as it broke her heart all over again to think about it. It had been the only way.

"He said he would. But you know how impatient I am. I had to come myself, just in case he couldn't talk sense into you."

There was a tentative knock at the door, followed by a more insistent one. Caroline crossed back to the door to open it, where Dora and Millie waited on the other side.

"How are you?" Millie asked immediately. "Are you hurt?"

"I'm perfectly fine," Caroline said through gritted teeth. She loved her friends, but this constant insinuation that she'd been knocked over the head and dragged off against her will was too much.

"We've been so worried," Dora said as she stepped forward to hug Caroline.

Caroline's irritation melted as she wrapped her arms around her friend. These women meant everything to her. Of course they were concerned, especially after she'd left so suddenly.

"I'm so sorry to have made you worry," Caroline said, looking into Dora's dark eyes. "But I'm fine, I promise."

"Are you ready to give up this nonsense and come back home with us?" Penny asked, her hands on her hips.

Caroline sank onto the pretty rose-colored settee. "I'm returning to Boston."

"I don't understand," Millie said. "You worked so hard to leave. Why would you return?"

"It's . . . hard to explain." Caroline studied her hands clasped on her lap.

"We have until six o'clock," Dora said, sitting next to her. "Mr. McFarland drove us up here in the buckboard. Mrs. Ruby convinced him. She misses you as much as we do."

Caroline glanced at Penny, who stood next to Dora.

"You should tell them. What does it matter now, if you won't be a Gilbert Girl any longer?" Penny said, a slight edge to her voice.

Caroline knew her friend hadn't forgiven her yet for leaving her post. Hopefully that would come with time. She drew a deep breath and told Millie and Dora about Thomas.

"You sly girl!" Millie said. "How did you hide that from us so well?"

"How can you leave him?" Dora asked. "Especially now, when he's so close to being free?"

Tears pricked Caroline's eyes but she refused to let them go any farther. "*I'm* the one who isn't free."

The three other girls blinked at her.

She drew a deep breath. "You know my family wants me to marry a man in Boston. But I didn't tell you that it's a formal engagement. And it isn't one I could simply break off. My father and I signed a contract—I would marry and this man would save my family's company." As soon as the words were out of her mouth, Caroline felt as if she'd finally come up for air after swimming in the ocean for months. The secret had clung to her for so long, it was a relief to be rid of it.

"Oh," Dora said softly, while Millie and Penny simply gaped at her.

"Whyever didn't you say anything?" Penny finally asked. "It isn't as if that's some dark secret."

Caroline squeezed her eyes shut. "Because he's a terrible man. He's much, much older. He's been married twice before and both of his wives died . . . strangely. And before their deaths, they often bowed out of parties and dinners, but when they came, they were quiet and tried to hide bruises with powder and rouge." She opened her eyes to meet her friends'. "I was scared. If I refused, my father wouldn't receive the money he needed to keep the company going. And . . . I was afraid Mr. Wiltshire would hurt me if I said no."

Dora reached for her hand. Millie's mouth hung open. But Penny—Penny was angry.

"Why did your father allow this?" she demanded.

"He refused to believe anything unseemly about Mr. Wiltshire."

"I'd like to meet your father," Penny muttered.

"But why do you want to go back now?" Millie asked.

"I'm tired of running. Of hiding. And I'm tired of pretending my heart is my own to give away, when it isn't." The tears threatened again, and Caroline steeled herself. It was no use crying now. She'd made her decision. Thomas was already on his way to Barrett Mountain. And she'd be home in Boston next week.

"This Mr. Wiltshire couldn't do anything if you were already married," Penny said bluntly.

Caroline looked back down at her hands, one of them still in Dora's. "That won't happen. And how is it fair to burden any man with this danger? If Mr. Wiltshire found out I married someone else, I'm afraid he'd come after us both."

"One who loves you would gladly take that risk," Dora said, squeezing Caroline's hand.

Her heart nearly shattered. Could Thomas have been that man? She would never know now. It was too late. She had let him go. *It's better for him*, she thought. He didn't deserve to be tied to such a mess.

No, her place was in Boston, where she would do her duty to her family. She wouldn't know love again, but maybe she could find her own sense of peace.

If you survive, the voice in her head reminded her.

"You can't return," Millie said. "If you marry that man, you'll never be happy. And . . . and . . ."

"Your life will be in danger," Penny finished for her.

"I'll be fine. My family has a summer home in Newport. I can always go there if I need to get away." Caroline spoke the words even if she didn't believe them. "My father's company will survive."

"Who *cares* about his company?" Penny threw up her hands. "What about you? What about the rest of your life?"

"It's already determined." She felt like a husk of herself; all of her emotions had gone, and all that was left was a dutiful daughter and fiancée. Maybe that would be how she survived.

Before Penny could speak another word of protest, the door opened, and in walked Quentin. If he was surprised to see the group of women surrounding his sister, he didn't show it. Instead, he smiled and inclined his head to each one of them in turn as Caroline introduced them.

"Please," he said. "Join us for dinner downstairs."

"Our driver is returning to the hotel at six," Penny said.

"Then you must be going." Caroline stood and ushered her friends to the door, even though it was still over an hour until six o'clock.

Penny glowered at her. "Think about what we said."

"Please," Dora said.

"It isn't too late," Millie added.

Caroline hugged them each in turn, and when she shut the door, Quentin fixed her with a question mark in his expression.

"It's nothing," she said quickly. "I must rest before dinner." She retreated to her room, determined to focus on the future and not the past.

Despite what her friends said, it was indeed too late. Not that it mattered, though. She was born into a certain kind of life, and it was time she stopped running from it.

Even if it meant she wouldn't have much life left.

Chapter Twenty-nine

The Cañon City jail was not a welcoming place. It was warm enough, and Thomas was thankful the only other occupant at the moment was a man sleeping off a drunken night in the next cell, but the only window let in just a sliver of light and the bars served as a constant reminder of his fate.

He'd only been in here since late the night before. He'd left willingly, and no one in the Crest Stone Hotel lobby had been any the wiser. He couldn't have taken McFarland or anyone else seeing him so demeaned. They'd immediately ridden north, and several hours later, Thomas found himself installed in this jail cell. He hadn't seen Frank since they'd arrived. Presumably, he'd run off to telegraph Barrett Mountain and celebrate. Thomas had been mostly alone, minus the drunk next door and one of the Cañon City deputies, who checked in on them from time to time.

His stomach rumbled as he lay on his back along the narrow bench in the back of the cell. He hadn't eaten anything since the meager breakfast the deputy had brought him this morning. There was no sense of time in this place, but he guessed it was growing close to evening. Although what did time matter now? Everything he'd hoped for was gone. He hadn't gotten his proof. Caroline was likely on a train north to Denver by now. All of his work in Crest Stone was for naught.

His future was a prison or the noose.

Thomas sighed and pulled his hat down over his face. If only he'd left sooner, he might have what he needed to clear his name. If only he'd convinced Caroline . . . of what? His own worth? He snorted. That was unlikely. He didn't even know why she was returning home to a future she'd said she didn't want, willingly leaving behind everything she'd worked for here. None of it made any sense—this woman who'd gone from kind and warm to cold and haughty. He wished he'd been able to speak with her again, put his hands on her shoulders, break through that wall of ice she'd formed around herself, and demand to know *why*.

Don't waste yourself on moneyed women, son. His father's advice from years ago echoed in his head. He'd followed it gratefully over the years, until now. But Caroline was different, or so he'd thought. Even when she'd been so cold to him in the dining room, there was something sad that hung about her like a shadow. As if she was forcing herself to act that way. As if she felt—as Thomas did now—that her fate was inevitable.

He sat up. That would explain why she'd changed character so quickly. But was it true or was it his own wishful thinking? After all, she'd blinded him to his own father's advice, advice he'd heeded for years after seeing what his mother had done.

He slammed his hat on the bench. He'd never know the answers to these questions. Instead, he was doomed to let them spin in his mind for years while he was locked away for simply defending himself and the company's goods. Maybe he'd be lucky if they let him hang instead.

"Drexel." Rayburn's voice, sounding as if it had shorn the edges off itself from speaking too much for too long, echoed through the room.

Thomas sighed. Exactly what he needed right now—Frank Rayburn crowing again about his grand deeds and Thomas's imminent demise. Thomas had heard enough of that on the ride up from Crest Stone.

"I trust you've found yourself at home here." The man stopped in front of his cell, hat in his hand. He was dressed well in what looked like a new suit and a black tie knotted around his neck.

Thomas didn't reply. Instead, he stood, leaning with one hand against the bars on the side of the cell as if he didn't give one whit about Rayburn or the future he faced. He refused to give Rayburn that satisfaction.

"They'll bring you something to eat soon. Can't have you starving before your appearance in front of the judge. That'll be a day I've looked forward to for a long time." He eyed Thomas, who held his gaze. Rayburn watched him for a moment before tapping his hand against the bars. "Get a good night's sleep," he said with a slight grin.

Then he turned and left, reaching into his pocket for something that glinted in the dying light.

Thomas let out a lungful of air. What he'd give to punch Frank in the face, just once. Yet another thing he'd never get the opportunity to do.

He'd just sunk back down onto the bench when the deputy called down the short row of cells. "Drexel! You got visitors."

That made him stand back up. He didn't know a soul in Cañon City, much less anyone who'd visit him. He clutched the bars and tried to peer down toward the deputy.

Not a few seconds later, three ladies appeared.

And Thomas was lost for words.

Chapter Thirty

The hotel restaurant was much more grand than Caroline had expected. She and Quentin had arrived first, but it wasn't long before their dining companions joined them.

"Ah! Mayor, good to see you again." Quentin rose to greet the four men who had arrived. He introduced the mayor to Caroline, along with the owner of the largest mercantile in town, and the local sheriff, Ben Young.

"Pleased to meet you, Miss Beauchamp." Sheriff Young inclined his head, the star on his jacket winking in the gas light. "This is Sheriff Frank Rayburn. He's here briefly from a mining town farther north." He gestured to the fourth man.

Caroline stifled a gasp. It was the tall, broad man who'd saved her and Penny from the drunken man at the small restaurant several weeks ago. The man who was looking for Thomas.

He apparently recognized her too. His eyes lit up and he smoothed his greased-down rust-colored hair before extending a hand to her. Caroline steadied her breathing and allowed him to take her hand.

"I believe we've met before, Miss Beauchamp," he said, letting her hand go.

She shoved it into her lap, thankful for the white gloves she hadn't yet removed. "Yes, we have, Sheriff. Thank you again for your assistance."

Quentin looked at her quizzically, but before she could explain, Sheriff Rayburn did it for her.

"They let you run about this . . . *town* without a chaperone?" Quentin asked when the sheriff had finished.

Caroline clenched her hands in her lap. Trust her brother to latch on to the one unimportant thing in that entire explanation. "The McFarlands trusted us to keep together and only visit appropriate establishments."

Quentin still frowned, and she knew nothing she could say about the Gilbert Company would satisfy him. He was determined to believe the worst. It was hard to fault him, though, when the only thing he was familiar with was Boston society.

"I am happy to say," Sheriff Rayburn said as the men sat, "that just yesterday I arrested the outlaw I told you about, Miss Beauchamp."

Caroline froze. It couldn't be. She must have heard him wrong.

"Miss Beauchamp?" he said.

"Are you well?" the mayor asked from next to her.

She forced herself to speak. "Yes, I am, thank you. I apologize, Sheriff. What were you saying?"

He smiled benevolently from across the table, as if she were a child who needed everything explained slowly. "Remember I told you and your friend I was searching for one Tom the Cat?"

She nodded. Her throat was parched, but she didn't dare reach for the glass of water that sat in front of her. Her hands were shaking too hard.

"I journeyed to your hotel, the Crest Stone, I believe? And there he was, working for the place, plain as day."

"Unbelievable," Quentin said. "You made the right decision, Caroline, leaving that place. Had we known you were there, living alongside such ruffians . . ." He trailed off, shaking his head.

"I wouldn't fault the company, Mr. Beauchamp," the local sheriff said from farther down the table. He gave Caroline a quick smile. "I've heard they hold the highest standards for their employees. I've no doubt that man lied his way into working there."

"What—" Caroline stopped and pulled in a breath to steady her nerves. "What will happen to him now? This man you caught, I mean."

"You shouldn't concern yourself with such matters," Quentin said. He looked at her as if she'd lost her mind, inquiring after a criminal.

"I'll transport him to the court in Denver where a judge will decide his fate," Sheriff Rayburn said, ignoring Quentin's comment. "It's likely he'll hang for murder and thievery."

Hang. The word sounded almost hollow, as if the meaning had disappeared from the middle of it. *Hang. Hang. Hang.* Caroline dropped her eyes to the table setting in front of her. The waiter arrived at that moment, which, happily, distracted the men. Irritation shot through Caroline when Quentin ordered for her, even though he'd always done so in Boston. But Caroline was no longer the same girl she'd been in Boston. Thomas had been right—the old rules didn't apply here. She'd pushed him away. And now Thomas could likely die for protecting himself and the company he'd worked for. Caroline's heart ached with a ferocity she hadn't felt since her father had told her she'd be marrying Mr. Wiltshire.

The conversation veered into business matters, with Quentin inquiring about the town's needs for various goods. Caroline watched Sheriff Rayburn across from her. He was jovial, unconcerned that an innocent man might die. Of course, he didn't know the truth.

She couldn't let this happen. She couldn't simply return to Boston and leave Thomas here to face this alone. But what could she do? She could hardly flounce down to the town jail and pay him a visit. Quentin would never allow it.

She wrapped a hand around her water glass, trying to think of something—anything—that would help. Something shiny glinted through the water, blinding her momentarily. Caroline glanced away, blinking away the burst of light in her eyes. When she turned back, it was still there, though less bright. What was that? She followed the light to the lamp on the table that sat just to the right between herself and Sheriff Rayburn. The sheriff had his left hand resting on the table. Something gold glinted from his little finger. It caught the light from the lamp and sent it through Caroline's water glass.

Caroline squinted at the ring, as a memory Thomas had shared with her tumbled through her mind. It was almost impossible. After all, many successful men wore gold rings, and the sheriff hadn't impressed her in any way that would indicate he was of a lesser moral character than he appeared to be. Still . . . Thomas had said the man was present right after he'd shot the sheriff. He'd discounted the idea that the now-sheriff could have been the one who'd stolen the money, since he'd had no way to transport it. But there was a possibility, as slim as it was. And if she didn't pursue it, she knew she couldn't live with herself.

"Excuse me, Sheriff," she said quietly over the mercantile owner going on about fabrics and weapons.

Sheriff Rayburn turned his gaze from the men to Caroline. "Miss Beauchamp?"

"I was admiring your ring," she said slowly to keep her voice from trembling. "May I see it?"

"Of course." He pulled it from his finger and handed it across the table.

It felt heavy in her hand, as if it were filled with secrets. There was a small filigree that wrapped around the band. She searched her memory for what Thomas said about his father's ring, and came up with nothing, except that it was gold and was worn on the pinky. She turned it sideways, looking along the inside of the band. And there, small and worn but still legible, were three letters.

TJD.

She almost gasped, but kept her face impassive. She didn't know Thomas's father's name, but it was likely they shared one. She forced herself to hand the ring back to the sheriff, who replaced it on his finger. "It looks old. Is it an heirloom?"

"No. It's something I found," he said, looking up at her. "Someone clearly didn't care much for it if they couldn't be bothered to keep it in their possession."

"Clearly," she repeated as her mind raced.

This was Thomas's proof, right there on Sheriff Rayburn's finger.

Chapter Thirty-one

The man in the next cell snored as Caroline's friends from the hotel crowded around Thomas's bars. He assumed Caroline would be in Denver by now, if not already on a train east to Boston. Thomas couldn't land on a reason why her friends would be here, in the Cañon City jail, standing outside his cell.

"Ladies," he said before fixing his eyes on Miss May, the only one of the three with whom he'd ever spoken with at length before. "Might I ask what I've done to deserve this unexpected visit?" He was afraid to ask how they knew where to find him.

"We're here because of Caroline. She's not thinking straight." Miss May tapped the side of her head.

"I never had the opportunity to see her." He gripped the bars. "But you spoke with her? Is she still in town?"

"Yes," Miss May said as if he were slow in the head. "I couldn't piece together why you said you'd come to talk to her but fail to do so. I asked around and discovered you'd been arrested. So . . . here we are."

"What did Caroline say?" He'd hoped she would come if she knew he was here. But she hadn't. That could only mean the worst.

"She doesn't know you're in jail. We didn't find out until after we left her hotel. We were trying to talk sense into her, but she won't hear it. She insists she's better off if she marries this Mr. Wiltshire her family promised her to."

Thomas swallowed hard. "That was the entire reason she left home. None of this makes any sense." He turned and crossed the small cell, running a hand through his hair. Why would she change her mind? It was exactly what he'd hoped to ask her when he saw her. Even if she didn't want him, she couldn't marry someone she didn't love.

Unless she did love that Mr. Wiltshire.

He felt ill. It *couldn't* be possible. Not with how despondent she'd looked when she told Thomas about her father's plans for her marriage.

"I can tell you she certainly doesn't love this Mr. Wiltshire." It was as if Miss May had read his mind.

He let out a huff of air. He'd been ready to push these bars aside barehanded and board a train to Boston, all for the pleasure of knocking this Wiltshire to the ground. "Then why would she agree to return home and marry him? Did she tell you?"

"Yes." Miss May pushed her lips together before speaking again. "Well . . ." Miss May looked to the girl with red hair and a ruffled yellow dress. He'd never seen her at a loss for words.

"He's evil," the other girl said.

"My mother would say he's the devil come down to earth," the quiet girl with the olive complexion said. She hid just behind the other two, and he had the feeling that when she spoke, it was important to listen.

Miss May drew a deep breath and turned to face Thomas again. She clutched a small reticule between her hands, which she squeezed as she spoke. "This man has been married twice before. Both of his wives met untimely deaths. Caroline indicated she was afraid he might hurt you if he knew of her fondness for you."

Thomas fixed his jaw. "I need out of here," he said, mostly to himself. He was useless inside this cell.

"That's why we came. We tried to talk her out of going. After all, she'll always have a place at the Crest Stone. But she wouldn't hear of it. It's almost as if she's resigned herself to this horrible fate to save her father's company and to protect you." Miss May wrapped a gloved hand around one of the bars. "What are your feelings toward Caroline?"

It was quiet save for the sleeping man's breathing as Thomas caught Miss May's eyes. How *did* he feel?

He'd told himself she'd used him as a passing fancy, until the novelty of working on the frontier wore off for her. That she was like his mother, concerned only for her own comfort. But it wasn't true, and he knew this, deep down. Those were only things he'd told himself to hide his own hurt, to push her memory away so he could move on with his life. So he could face years in prison, or death, without her ghost haunting him.

"I . . ." He closed his eyes briefly. When he opened them, each of her friends was looking at him, waiting. "I love her."

Miss May smiled in triumph, and the other two girls followed suit.

He shifted uncomfortably before forcing his mind to work toward the practical instead of dwelling on what he'd just admitted. "But I can't get out of here. I'm due to a judge in Denver for—" He cut himself off. He didn't know how much Caroline had told Miss May of his past.

But Miss May let her hands fall to her sides and stepped forward. "Caroline told me your story. If she believes you, then I do too, despite what I might have said to you before. I was simply looking out for my friend's heart, and I thought you were nothing more than a rake."

Thomas wasn't entirely certain what to say to that. "Thank you, I suppose."

"Perhaps if we spoke to Caroline again?" the redhead in the yellow dress said. "If we told her what you said . . . if that's all right with you, sir, I mean. Maybe she'd agree to come see you."

Thomas rubbed his face with his hand, hoping to erase any sign of embarrassment. "Anything to keep her from leaving with her brother. You can tell her I'm on my deathbed, if that's what it takes."

Miss May gave him another smile, and he had the feeling he'd just won her hard-earned approval.

"We've already delayed poor Mr. McFarland," the quieter girl said.

Miss May waved her hand. "He'll wait longer. It's not as if he'll leave us here."

"You're right," the girl in the yellow dress said. "Let's hurry."

Miss May placed a hand against the bars. "We'll return, with Caroline. I promise."

"Just don't let her leave town," he said. He watched them retreat. He'd gladly face the noose if he could keep Caroline safe. And tell her he loved her.

Chapter Thirty-two

"I believe I don't feel well at all." Caroline placed a hand to her cheek as she spoke.

The men across the table all looked concerned. Perhaps she could consider a life on the stage.

"I'll escort you upstairs." Quentin rose and placed his napkin on the table. "Excuse me, gentlemen. I'll return as soon as I see my sister safely to our rooms."

The men all stood to murmur their good nights and well wishes, and in seconds, Quentin had his arm through Caroline's. He walked her a bit faster than was necessary through the dining room and up the hotel stairs.

"I'm sorry to be a bother," she said. "I know you need to speak with them about business."

"You're no bother," he said. They stopped outside their second floor door as he fished for the key in his pocket. The door unlocked with a click, and he pushed it open. "Get some rest, and perhaps you'll feel better in the morning."

She nodded and took a step inside.

Quentin placed a hand on the door. "I'm happy you've come to realize this nonsense of being a waitress is just that. The family will be overjoyed you're returning to us. We've all missed you greatly." He leaned forward and placed a kiss on her head before giving her a smile and closing the door.

Caroline stood there for a moment as his footsteps retreated, a hand to her heart. Her brother wasn't a terrible person. He truly believed the rumors about Mr. Wiltshire were just that—rumors. He wanted the best for her, and in his short-sighted Boston way, he believed the best was marriage to a successful man with a good name.

And for a while, Caroline had forced herself to believe the same, even as she pushed the waves of fear for her very life aside. But seeing that ring had been akin to being struck by lightning.

A life in Boston was *not* what she wanted, Wiltshire or not. She wanted to live, she wanted to feel useful, and she wanted to be happy. And working at the Crest Stone had made her happy. Being with Thomas had exceeded her wildest dreams.

And now she had the proof he needed to save his life.

She didn't know what to do about the contract or the fear that Thomas's life could be in danger if Mr. Wiltshire found out about him. But she didn't have time to ponder those problems right now. Caroline rushed to her room and withdrew a pearl-colored cloak from the wardrobe. She flew out the door and down the stairs, taking care to pull up the hood before she passed the entrance to the dining room.

Outside on the street, the temperature had dropped considerably. Caroline stood there shivering as she realized she had no idea where the jail was.

"Caroline!"

It couldn't be. They were supposed to have left already. But no . . . there were her friends, approaching from the left. Caroline ran to meet them.

"You must come with us!" Millie said, her face flushed.

"Where?" Caroline asked, and then shook her head. "I can't. I need to get to Thomas. I found the proof he needs."

"That's where we were going to bring you!" Penny said, grabbing her arm. "He has something he needs to tell you."

"Wait, did you say you have proof? What sort of proof?" Dora asked as they hurried down the wooden sidewalk, past all manner of people—gentlemen, a few ladies, cowboys, miners.

"Yes! I don't have it with me, but I saw it. It'll prove that Thomas is innocent of all the charges levied against him." Caroline picked up her pace until she was nearly dragging Penny down the sidewalk. Her brother would certainly disapprove of the spectacle she was making of herself, but then again, he also wouldn't approve of her ultimate destination.

It wasn't long before they reached the sheriff's office and jail. Penny pushed the door open as if she were expected.

Inside, a single lamp glowed in the darkness, illuminating a desk covered in papers and a pair of boots. The boots were attached to legs that belonged to a man Caroline presumed was a sheriff's deputy. He was fast asleep.

Penny shook her head. “Let’s go. We know where he is.” She led the way across the long and narrow room to the rear of the building, where she pushed open another door.

This next room was lined with several jail cells. A few lamps hung from the walls, and Penny strode through their flickering light to the last cell where a man stood against the bars.

Thomas.

Caroline gasped at seeing him trapped like this. His hands clenched the bars as his eyes drank her in. She stood rooted to the floor. She wanted nothing more than to run to him and entwine her fingers with his, but she’d hurt him. Badly.

“You came,” he said, his voice rough.

“Of course I did.” She could’ve smacked herself. There was no “of course” about it, not after what she’d said to him. “I’m . . . I’m sorry. For pushing you away so suddenly. For running.” Her friends stood behind her, and she was thankful for their presence. With them by her side, she wouldn’t run again.

His Adam’s apple bobbed. “Did they tell you what I said?”

Caroline furrowed her eyebrows. “No, I don’t believe so.”

The smile that cut across his face warmed her heart. “And you came anyway.” He held a hand out through the bars.

Caroline’s body nearly melted in relief. He’d forgiven her. She stepped forward and grasped his hand with both of hers. “I found it,” she said softly.

He tilted his head, questioning.

“The proof you need.”

“How? Where is it? *What* is it?” His hand tightened around hers as the questions flowed.

“It’s your father’s ring. Remember, the one you told me about?”

He nodded.

“I saw it tonight, on Sheriff Rayburn’s hand. It has initials engraved on the inside of the band—TJD. That’s it, isn’t it?”

His eyes widened. “It is. But how could he have . . .?”

“I don’t know. What should we do?”

He rubbed his free hand across the scruff on his chin. “The local sheriff. Ben Young. We need to inform him.”

"He's at dinner with my brother and Sheriff Rayburn," Caroline said. "How can we draw him away?"

"An emergency," Penny supplied. "One of us can approach him in some sort of distress and lead him here, without the others. I'll go now."

She was already halfway down the aisle toward the door when Thomas spoke. "Fetch McFarland too, if you please. I have a feeling we're going to need him."

Millie took Dora's hand. "We'll do that."

Caroline squeezed Thomas's hand. "I don't want to leave you, but I want to ensure this all goes as planned. I'll follow Penny and keep my distance."

"But your brother . . . ?"

"I won't let him see me."

Thomas lifted her hands to his lips and placed a gentle kiss on her knuckles. "Come back to me."

Caroline's heart pounded at his touch. How had she thought she could give him up so easily? "Nothing will stop me." She unwound her hands from Thomas's and walked as fast as she could to the door.

Thomas would be free tonight, and no one would get in the way of that. For once she wasn't running away. Instead, she was running headlong toward something. And someone.

Chapter Thirty-three

Waiting was agonizing. Thomas paced the cell back and forth. His blasted neighbor was still asleep and he'd begun to wonder if the man was ever going to wake up. To pass the time, he relived the moment when Caroline came into view and took his hand, over and over.

She had no idea how he felt, and she'd come anyway. She *was* the woman he'd thought she was.

His heart soared until he remembered he wasn't free yet. There were still so many potential pitfalls. Rayburn could hide the ring. The sheriff could choose not to believe him, despite the evidence. The sheriff could simply refuse to come with Miss May. Caroline's brother could spot her and refuse to let her leave their hotel room until it was time to board the train to Denver.

He shook his head. That last one wouldn't matter. If he was out of this cell in time, he'd beat the door down until he was with her again. They'd both owned up to their fates, and now they were changing them and—hopefully—creating a world in which they both could live unbound from their pasts.

A commotion at the door drew him to the bars again. He squinted through the lamplight, trying to see the cause and praying it was Miss May returned with the sheriff.

"This is utter nonsense," a man's voice carried down the row of cells as the door opened.

"The girl's had us," another man said.

"Sheriff, there ain't been an escape," the deputy's voice echoed down the cells.

"*Please* come with me. We're almost there," Miss May's voice said.

They came into view at just that moment, a parade of irritated gentlemen and an insistent young woman. Thomas took a step back. He'd expected just the local sheriff, but she'd somehow brought him along with three men he'd never seen before—and Sheriff Frank Rayburn, who stared at him coldly. The moment Rayburn turned away, Thomas glanced at the man's left hand. There, on his little finger, was a gold band that hadn't been there earlier, when Rayburn had arrested him and brought him here. His heart nearly stopped. Rayburn had stolen the money. Thomas didn't know how, but that was the only way he could've gotten his hands on that ring, and it explained why he would've hidden it from Thomas.

"Young lady, we left a perfectly good meal to aid the sheriff with preventing an escape from his jail," an imposing man in an expensive black suit said. "However, neither of these men—" He waved his hand at Thomas and the drunk, who was, finally, awake. "—appears to be on the verge of forcing their way out from behind these bars."

The girl turned to Thomas, and just as he was about to speak, the door opened again and the crowd in front of his cell turned to see who it was.

"Miss Beauchamp?" one of the men said.

"Caroline!" A younger man with hair the color of Caroline's pushed his way through the group. "This is no place for you. Why aren't you resting?"

Thomas pressed himself against the bars. Just catching a glimpse of her gave him courage. She glanced at him as she arrived. "I apologize. We didn't mean to pull all of you away from your meal."

"We?" The younger man, most likely Caroline's brother, said. His gaze swung to Caroline's friend. "I recognize you now. You were visiting my sister earlier today. Miss . . .?"

"May," the girl filled in.

Mr. Beauchamp looked at her for a moment before turning back to his sister. "Caroline, do you or Miss May care to explain why you interrupted dinner with this nonsense?"

Caroline stepped forward just as the door opened yet again. It had to be McFarland—at least Thomas hoped it was.

Beauchamp turned a frustrated shade of red. "And now who is this? Really, Caroline, this is ridiculous."

The other two girls entered the tableau in front of Thomas's cell with McFarland. Miss May looked ready to answer Beauchamp with something distinctly impolite, but Caroline spoke first.

"This is Mr. McFarland, the manager of the Crest Stone Hotel, and two dear friends of mine, Miss Sinclair and Miss Reynolds." Caroline's voice was strong, and she glanced at Thomas.

He gave her a reassuring smile, even though his guts were twisted in a knot. Caroline turned away quickly, but not before her brother caught the look between them. His eyes narrowed slightly as he seemed finally to notice the man in the cell in front of him.

"Gentlemen, I believe we've been tricked," he said, turning toward the company gathered behind him.

"No! No, please. I'm the one who gathered you all here. Although, sirs, I apologize. I only meant to call for the sheriff and Mr. McFarland." Caroline gave them all a smile that had to have melted their hearts. "Mayor, gentlemen, if you'd like to return to your dinner, please do."

"I admit I'm curious," one of the men said. "But, Mr. Beauchamp, I'll let you sort this out. Perhaps we can finish our conversation another time?"

Caroline's brother nodded and shook the man's hand, clearly distracted. The two men Thomas didn't recognize retreated toward the door, leaving only the girls, McFarland, Mr. Beauchamp, and the two sheriffs.

"Sheriff," Caroline said to Sheriff Young. "I have evidence that this man in your jail is innocent of the charges laid against him."

Rayburn crossed his arms. "Miss Beauchamp, I've been searching for Drexel all over this territory for months. I believe you've been misled."

"I have not, sir." She lifted her chin and gave him a look that could melt ice. If Thomas hadn't already realized how much he loved this woman, the look she gave Rayburn now would've certainly done it.

"I acted only to defend myself," Thomas said.

"After you stole thousands of dollars in company pay. Or have you forgotten?" Rayburn gave him a brief glance before continuing. "Gentlemen, I'm sorry for this interruption. Perhaps we should return to dinner?"

"I'd like to hear Miss Beauchamp out," McFarland said, his own arms crossed against the breadth of his stomach. "The girl went through an awful lot of trouble to gather us all here."

"It's clear this outlaw has twisted her mind," Rayburn said.

"He's done no such thing," Caroline snapped.

Her brother stepped forward, laying a hand on her arm. "You aren't feeling well."

She threw off his arm. "I'm feeling perfectly fine, Quentin. And I'd appreciate it if you'd stop treating me as if I'm some delicate thing that will break under the slightest provocation."

His eyes widened, and Thomas smothered a chuckle. Despite the gravity of the situation, seeing his Caroline put her brother in his place was quite the sight.

"McFarland," Beauchamp finally said, sputtering. "I don't know what kind of establishment you're running down there in that valley, but my sister—"

"Your sister is a hard worker and quite trustworthy, I've been told," McFarland said. "Please, Miss Beauchamp, continue."

"Thank you," Caroline said. "As I was saying, Mr. Drexel here stole nothing, and he shot at the sheriff to prevent the man from shooting him, after the sheriff had attempted to steal the entire payroll. He didn't mean to cause the man's death."

Rayburn scoffed. "That's ridiculous. He's filled your head with lies, girl. What other pretty words did he tell you so you'd let him do as he pleased?"

Caroline's jaw dropped as Thomas slammed his hands against the bars. "You shut your mouth, or I—"

"You'll what, Drexel? What are you going to do from in there?" Rayburn sneered at him. The man was lucky Thomas couldn't get to him.

"How dare you imply my sister is anything less than virtuous?" Beauchamp's face had gone bright red.

"I suggest you apologize for impugning this good woman's reputation," McFarland said, an edge to his voice.

"I would if it wasn't likely the truth. This man's nothing but a thief and a murderer," Rayburn said.

Thomas wrapped his hands around the bars, anger and frustration building as he couldn't do a thing from inside this cell.

"Caroline," Beauchamp said, still tomato red, his hands clenched at his sides. "Please tell me you haven't entertained anything from this man."

Caroline pushed her shoulders back and lifted her chin. "If you please, gentlemen, I'd like to continue."

Her brother did not look appeased, but he said nothing.

"Your ring, Sheriff," she said, gesturing at Rayburn's hand. "You were kind enough to show it to me at dinner. It belongs to Mr. Drexel."

Rayburn laughed, but there was a sharp edge to the sound. Thomas smiled just a little. Rayburn had been caught, and he knew it.

"I suppose he told you that," Rayburn said. "Another lie. I had it made in Denver."

Caroline's eyes narrowed. "You said you found it."

"You misunderstood."

"I don't believe she did," Thomas said. "There's an inscription on the inside of the band."

"And?" Rayburn said.

"What does it say?" Thomas dropped his hands to his sides, waiting as Rayburn blustered.

"I've had this for years. How would I remember such a thing?"

"TJD. Thomas Joseph Drexel. My father's initials."

Rayburn locked gazes with him. And if hellfire was here on Earth, it was certainly in the sheriff's eyes right now.

"Let's get on with it," Sheriff Young said. "Just remove the ring and let's have the answer."

Rayburn remained still, before finally pulling the ring from his finger and handing it to Young, who held it up to the light.

"TJD." Young held the ring in his hand and turned to Thomas. "You're correct, but I'm afraid that doesn't prove anything except that Sheriff Rayburn found your ring somewhere back in that mining town."

Thomas didn't dare hope too much. He'd waited for so long, and now, here he was, on the verge of being free. "I lost that ring in a lockbox. The same lockbox of money that went missing that day."

"And how would we know that's true?" Sheriff Young asked.

Rayburn watched Thomas, a challenge written all over his face, while Caroline smiled at him encouragingly.

"Because a few railroad employees helped me search for it after we filled the box with money and closed it up. We came to the conclusion that the ring had fallen into the box. I'd planned to look inside for it after we'd delivered the box to the mine office. You see," Thomas said, his voice even, "that ring was the only thing I have left from my father."

Rayburn swallowed. "That proves nothing."

"On the contrary," Sheriff Young said. "If the witnesses tell the same story, it proves Drexel here didn't steal the money."

"What are you implying?" Rayburn took a step forward.

"I believe you know," Young said. "It appears you took that money, Rayburn."

Rayburn laughed, but no one else joined him.

"I'm afraid I'll need to place you under arrest," Young said. He waved a hand at the deputy, who unlocked a cell on the other side of the drunk man, who'd appeared to sober up and had been watching the scene before him play out with interest.

"You won't put me in that cell." Rayburn turned and pushed past McFarland and the women.

"Stop him!" Miss May shouted as Rayburn ran for the door.

Chapter Thirty-four

Caroline had grabbed the cell bars to keep from falling as Sheriff Rayburn pushed her aside. Mr. McFarland and Sheriff Young raced after Sheriff Rayburn, the deputy and Penny right behind them.

"I need out of here," Thomas nearly growled at the bars. "I swear, if they let him get away . . ."

Caroline placed a hand over one of his. "They won't."

His eyes met hers, and almost instantly, he calmed. "Thank you, for all of this."

Her breath stilled. "I refused to sit idly by once I saw that ring. It made me realize . . ."

Thomas covered her hand with his other one and smiled. The warmth from his touch radiated through her entire body, and all she wanted to do was melt away these bars that stood between them so she could find herself in his arms again.

Instead, her brother gripped her arm to pull her away. "I'll thank you kindly to remove your hands from my sister."

Caroline shook him off. Thomas didn't move his hands, but he studied Quentin from head to toe. "I mean her no disrespect. In fact . . ." His eyes returned to Caroline, and she wished they'd never leave her again. "She's everything to me. And all of me belongs to her, whether she knows it or not. You took my heart weeks ago, Caroline."

Every part of her went weak, with relief or happiness or surprise, she didn't know. Perhaps all of those at once. She could feel Dora and Millie move closer, while next to her, Quentin stiffened.

"How dare you," he said quietly.

But Thomas pretended not to hear. His entire focus was on her. When she lifted her hand to the bars, he grasped it. His touch warmed her body to its core. She never wanted to let him go.

"Caroline Beauchamp," he said. "I love you."

Her lips parted, and tears pricked at her eyes. Quentin made some sort of incomprehensible noise, while one of the girls behind her sighed. There was so much she wanted to say to Thomas—needed to say—but he continued before she could speak.

"I know I'm not much now. I don't have anything to give beyond my undying devotion to you. But I'll work hard until we have everything we ever dreamed we could—money, a business, a home as grand as you want it, anything that would make you happy. Because making you happy is all I want to do." He dropped to one knee, not letting go of her hands. "Please do me the honor of giving me your hand in marriage, my Caroline."

The tears fell fast now even as Millie squealed and grabbed on to Dora, while Quentin bristled.

"Are you mad?" her brother sputtered. "My sister isn't marrying some . . . some . . . ruffian outlaw. Our father won't hear of it."

"Father isn't here," Caroline said, her tears quickly turning into righteous indignation as Thomas stood. "And Thomas is no *ruffian outlaw*. He's an employee of the Gilbert Company who has just cleared his name from an unfortunate incident in which he was forced to defend himself."

Quentin stared down at her. "Who is his family? Where is he from? How will he provide for you in the manner you deserve?"

Caroline looked him right in the eyes, her chin lifted. "Why, Thomas is from Texas. I don't know his family, but he's been on his own since he was seventeen. And he'll provide for me just fine, thank you. Besides, I'm not afraid of a little hard work if it's needed."

Dora's arm encircled her waist, and Caroline leaned into her friend. Millie moved forward and said, "Caroline was named head waitress. She most certainly can take care of herself, if she needs to."

Quentin slammed a hand against the bars. "I *won't* hear of it. You're returning with me. Father's business, our entire livelihood, depends on your return." He turned to Thomas, his face twisted into a look of disgusted victory. "I don't suppose she shared her engagement with you. She's been betrothed to a man in Boston since April. She signed a contract, with our father's blessing."

Caroline felt as if all her joy in hearing Thomas's proclamation of love melted out of her with Quentin's revelation. While she'd told Thomas she was expected to marry Mr. Wiltshire, she hadn't been exactly forthright in sharing the extent of her commitment.

"I'm aware," Thomas said. Glancing down at Caroline, he added, "Miss May told me everything."

"I'm so sorry," she said to him, her voice barely a whisper. "I should have told you about the contract and the engagement. I . . ." She bit down on her lip, hoping to forestall more tears as her heart started to rip in two. "It's part of why I can't marry you now."

Thomas's face hardened. He held tightly to her hands. "Do you love him?"

Caroline laughed, short and heartless. "No. Not at all. I despise him. It's nothing more than a business transaction between him and my father to save my family's company."

"Contracts can be broken." Thomas turned to Quentin. "Particularly if they were signed under duress."

Quentin shifted, his eyes darting between Caroline and Thomas. "My sister was not under duress. She agreed with her own free will."

They both turned to Caroline. She wanted to shrink into the bars, into the safety of Thomas's arms. But now was a time to be brave. If Penny hadn't taken off after Sheriff Rayburn, Caroline knew she'd remind her of that. "I felt I had no choice. He is an evil man. Quentin, please, you don't hear the whispers among the ladies."

"Rumors, that's all," Quentin said.

"He's been married twice before," Millie piped up. "And both of his wives met ill ends."

If a look could wither a person, the one Quentin gave Millie would've done just that. But Millie simply stood taller as Dora held even more tightly to Caroline's waist.

"That's why I left," Caroline said to Thomas. "Yes, I was tired of hiding, but I was more afraid of what Mr. Wiltshire would do if he found out about you."

"You were trying to protect me." Thomas's voice cracked as he spoke.

Caroline nodded.

He rubbed a thumb over her hand, his eyes cast downward as if he didn't know what to say. Finally, he looked up, his entire soul bared in his eyes. "Do you want to return to Boston?"

"No. I want to stay here. With you," she added quietly. Her heart pounded, but she felt lighter than she had in months. The truth—all of it—was out there now. She couldn't blame Thomas if he no longer wanted her. It would hurt, and she wasn't sure if her heart would ever fully mend, but at least she'd be free of the trapped, and terrifying, life she would have lived if she'd returned to Boston.

"Then, sir, I believe you have your answer," Thomas said to Quentin before returning his attention to Caroline. "And my offer stands, if you'll have me."

She blinked at him, unbelieving. She'd kept so much of the truth from him. She'd hurt him badly when she left. "Are you certain?"

"I'd want you even if you'd married this Wiltshire and he divorced you," Thomas said. "Whatever hold that man—or your family—might have had on you is gone now, if you simply say the word. If he feels the need to come here and do me harm, rest assured I can defend the both of us." He glanced up at Quentin. "And you can relay that message on to him."

It was as if an anchor had been holding her to Boston, a chain she'd dragged with her all the way across the country. And now it was broken. She could leave all of that behind and start anew.

With Thomas.

She let one of his hands go and turned to face her brother. "Quentin, I love you and I love our family. But I will not go back to Boston, and I refuse to marry Mr. Wiltshire. My future is here, in the Colorado Territory. I'm breaking the engagement. You can tear up that contract."

Quentin breathed heavily, looking between her and Thomas. "You realize you're forcing your own family's company into the ground?"

"Is the company worth my life?"

Her brother stared at her, his jaw clenched. And said not a word.

"I'll read your silence as a no." Caroline turned to Thomas, who gave her a proud smile. "Thomas, I'd be honored to be your wife." As soon as the words were out of her mouth, she knew this was who she was meant for —this brave, rough-around-the edges man. Without him, her life would be empty.

Behind her, Quentin huffed. She heard him push past the girls and march toward the door.

Dora whispered something to Millie, and they silently followed, leaving Caroline and Thomas alone.

"If only these bars weren't here," he said as he brushed a hand over her hair, letting it linger on her cheek.

Caroline pressed her face into his palm. She'd missed him so much since she left Crest Stone. "It won't be long before you're finally free."

"Every moment I can't wrap my arms around you is a moment too long." He pulled her gently forward, until their faces were barely an inch apart.

"I could go see if the deputy left his keys on the desk."

"Don't you dare go anywhere." His breath was warm against her face.

She closed the tiny distance between them and met his lips. A million emotions stirred inside, all of them breaking free after being hidden, buried, ignored for so long. His fingers tightened around hers as she gripped one of the bars with her free hand.

When they finally broke apart, she felt as if she'd run for miles. "I could do that forever," she said, breathless.

A smile curved Thomas's lips as he looked down at her. "I'm not opposed to that idea. I don't suppose any minister will perform a wedding inside a jail?"

Caroline laughed until his lips crushed hers again. She'd never been happier to belong to someone, forever.

Epilogue

The first people through the door of the just-opened Crest Stone Mercantile and General Store were exactly who Caroline expected them to be. She stepped as gracefully as she could off the small stool behind the counter, where she'd been arranging the store's most expensive trinkets on shelving Thomas had built himself. Then she ran to her friends who stood in the doorway, their faces filled with awe as they took in the store and its variety of goods.

Caroline embraced them all in turn, and then the questions began.

"How did you arrange this all so nicely?" Dora asked as she ran a finger over a bolt of poplin. "It looks so different from when we lived here!"

"Is there anything that *isn't* in this store?" Millie added.

"Please say you have hair combs. I broke one this morning, and I don't think I can wait until after Sunday services to buy a new one," Penny said.

Caroline laughed. "We do have combs. And just about anything else you could want. Or we will, anyway, once more shipments arrive."

"Thanks to your brother," Thomas said as he came out of the storage room and wrapped his arms around her waist.

Caroline leaned back until her head rested comfortably in the crook of his shoulder.

Penny giggled. "We'll let you two be. Come on, girls. Let's see what this place has to offer." They disappeared down one of the aisles, and their exclamations of surprise over what they found echoed through the room.

Caroline rested for a moment in Thomas's arms. Now that Sheriff Rayburn was in Denver, awaiting trial, and Quentin had informed Mr. Wiltshire of Caroline's decision and Thomas's veiled threat, they'd both felt more free than they ever had before. It turned out that Sheriff Rayburn and the mining town's former sheriff, Ratterman, had planned to steal the company pay together and frame Thomas for the theft. They'd paid a couple of miners to hide with a wagon nearby, ready to run with the lockbox. When it all went wrong, Sheriff Rayburn simply cut his friend out of the plan and adjusted it so that Thomas would still take the blame.

"Happy?" Thomas asked, his chin resting on Caroline's head.

"More than I ever thought possible." Caroline turned to face her husband.

Husband. The word would never stop sounding marvelous and exciting. Despite the fact that they'd been married a few weeks now, Caroline felt just as she had on her wedding day. The minute Thomas had been let out of jail—or rather, several minutes, as they'd had to listen to Sheriff Young go on about how irresponsible and foolish Penny had been, following them when they went after Sheriff Rayburn—he'd found a minister in Cañon City who agreed to marry them in his own home. With only the girls and Mr. McFarland in attendance, they'd promised each other forever. Caroline didn't mind that it wasn't traditional. It was perfect for them, and neither of them wanted to spend another moment apart. She'd only wished her brother could have accepted her decision and been there for her. But he'd more than made up for it later.

"You've done wonders with this place," he said, touching his forehead to hers.

"You're the one who turned it into a store," she reminded him. "And a home."

After realizing there were other businessmen in Boston willing to help Beauchamp Imports survive without requiring a sacrifice from their family, Quentin had offered to provide collateral so Thomas could purchase the goods needed to sell in the store. The Gilbert Company had agreed to lease this old farmhouse to Thomas. The comfortable old home's parlor, dining room, and sitting room were now Crest Stone's first place of business aside from the hotel. Thomas and Caroline had taken the upstairs as their home, and Caroline planned to use the kitchen not only for their meals, but to prepare baked goods for sale in the store. There was still a lot of work to be done to the building, and many more goods to be added to the shelves, but in just a handful of weeks, they'd prepared enough to open the store.

"Just imagine how we'll see this town grow," Caroline said as Thomas dropped kisses along her forehead. "This is only the beginning, and you'll be part of it."

"*We'll* be part of it," he said before catching her chin in his hand and capturing her mouth with his.

There was nothing more Caroline could want.

THANK YOU FOR READING! Now you have to find out what adventure awaits Penny when Sheriff Ben Young comes to the Crest Stone Hotel and Restaurant. Their story, *Wild Forever*, is next, and is available here: http://bit.ly/WildForeverBook. For more *Gilbert Girls* news, sign up here: http://bit.ly/catsnewsletter I also give subscribers a free *Gilbert Girls* prequel novella (it tells the story of Mr. and Mrs. McFarland), sneak peeks at upcoming books, insights into the writer life, discounts and deals, the opportunity to join my advance reader team, inspirations, and so much more. I'd love to have *you* join the fun! You can also find me on Facebook at: http://bit.ly/CatonFacebook and on my website http://bit.ly/CatCahillAuthor

Turn the page to see a complete list of the books in the *Gilbert Girls* series.

Books in The Gilbert Girls series

Building Forever[1]
Running From Forever[2]
Wild Forever[3]
Hidden Forever[4]
Forever Christmas[5]

1. http://bit.ly/BuildingForeverbook
2. http://bit.ly/RunningForeverBook
3. http://bit.ly/WildForeverBook
4. http://bit.ly/HiddenForeverBook
5. http://bit.ly/ForeverChristmasBook

About the Author, Cat Cahill

A sunset. Snow on the mountains. A roaring river in the spring. A man and a woman who can't fight the love that pulls them together. The danger and uncertainty of life in the Old West. This is what inspires me to write. I hope you find an escape in my books!

I live with my family, my hound dog, and a few cats in Kentucky. When I'm not writing, I'm losing myself in a good book, planning my next travel adventure, doing a puzzle, attempting to garden, or wrangling my kids.

Manufactured by Amazon.ca
Bolton, ON

14471351R00085